Scam Man

Second Edition

Scam Man

Second Edition

Mike Faricy

Library of Congress Control Number: 2023914846
paperback ISBN: 978-1-962080-15-6
e-book ISBN: 978-1-962080-16-3

MJF Publishing books may be purchased for education, Business, or promotional use. For information on bulk purchases, please contact the author directly at mikefaricyauthor@gmail.com

Published by

MJF Publishing
https://www.mikefaricybooks.com

To Teresa
"Are you awake?"

Acknowledgments

I would like to thank the following people for their help and support:

Special thanks to my editors, Kitty, Donna and Rhonda for their hard work, cheerful patience and positive feedback.

I would like to thank Ann and Julie for their creative talent and not slitting their wrists or jumping off the high bridge when dealing with my Neanderthal computer capabilities.

Special thanks to Ann for her patience.

Last, I would like to thank family and friends for their encouragement and unqualified support. Special thanks to Maggie, Jed, Schatz, Pat, Av, Emily and Pat for not rolling their eyes, at least when I was there, and most of all, to my wife Teresa whose belief, support and inspiration has from day one, never waned.

One

Her name was really Amanda Jane, but she and everyone else referred to her as AJ. I met her a couple of weeks back at a friend's party, and we seemed to hit it off pretty well. I asked her out a couple of nights later.

On our first night out we'd gone to dinner at a small, very private little restaurant overlooking the river. Romantic, expensive, and both of us had a lovely time. We met at the restaurant. My experience had been there's no "dinner with benefits" on a first date. I get it. She was a classy gal and just getting to know me, so I was prepared. I got a text from her later that night saying, "Thanks."

On date number two, we grabbed a movie, some chick flick that she just loved, and I worked to stay awake. I kept cautiously checking my watch to see how much longer the torture would last, thinking more than once that the watch had stopped. We grabbed a glass of wine at an upscale bistro place after the movie. She mentioned the big important meeting she had the following morning after I suggested a drink at my place. So, I kissed her goodnight on her front porch steps and got the distinct impression that a grope was there for the taking, but it was only date number two, and her ultimate mission was to prove she wasn't a slut. Against my better judgment, I remained a gentleman. Mission accomplished.

Tonight was date number three. Experience suggested since she'd already proven she wasn't a slut, tonight would be the clincher. I'd pulled out all the stops since there was a better than even chance we might end up at my place. I laid in a couple of bottles of her favorite wine, put fresh flowers on the dining room table and in the den. I vacuumed, cleaned the bathroom, placed a scented candle next to the bathroom sink, hung clean towels, changed the sheets, and tossed the pile of laundry waiting to be washed into the basement.

I had eggs, bacon, sausage, and a cinnamon coffee cake set to go for breakfast. The coffee pot was programmed to start perking at eight tomorrow morning. Just in case, I'd even picked up a couple of different teas. All my bases were covered.

I made a reservation for 8:30 at Bobby's, a trendy little place just a five-minute drive from my house. I wanted to miss the hurry-up crowd, the folks who had somewhere else to go that night. We sat and laughed over a glass of wine for a good half hour before we even looked at the menu. AJ wore a slinky, low cut black dress that was so tight it looked like it was painted on. A little gold cross dangled intriguingly at the top of her cleavage, and I pictured myself at exactly the same spot in just a few hours. I ordered a soy sauce mushroom appetizer to share, and we took our time eating.

AJ nibbled a mushroom, then said, "Would you mind ordering dinner for me? I kind of, well, you know, I kind of like being told what to do." Then she raised her eyebrows in a suggestive way.

I ordered two sixteen-ounce steaks, medium-rare. I finished with a clean plate. AJ had the remaining two-thirds of her steak placed in a white Styrofoam takeout container. Our plates were cleared just after ten.

"May I interest either one of you in a dessert? Our special tonight is a delicious caramel custard made with free-range eggs and heavy cream from a local Minnesota dairy farm. I strongly recommend it," our waiter said, then flashed a charming smile.

"What do you think?" AJ asked. She brushed a sexy blonde lock back over her ear and bit her lower lip.

"If you want, or we could maybe go to my place for a nightcap, you know if you're feeling up to it." I crossed my fingers and counted to myself one, two, three, four—

"I better take a pass on dessert. The steak was delicious."

"Sir?"

"I think just the check when you have time."

"Actually, I'd love the dessert, but the nightcap might be more… interesting," she said, smiling.

I immediately wondered where in the hell the check was.

I got a lingering kiss just inside the restaurant before I held the door for her.

"Goodbye, thanks so much," she called to our waiter on the way out.

"Have a fun night, folks," he replied.

"I plan to," AJ said and made a beeline for my car parked at the curb.

I held the door for her, and she gave me another kiss before she slid into the passenger seat. Once I started the car, she said, "Would you mind if I turned the channel on your radio? There's a station that plays real romantic music until midnight on Fridays. Really gets me in the mood."

"Oh, yeah, great idea. I love romantic music."

She hummed along with the song as we raced to my place. As I drove, she gently rubbed her index finger up and down my neck. I made the five-minute drive in just under three and pulled to the curb.

"I've been dreaming about this all week. I really want to see… your place," she said. Then she undid her seat belt and waited for me to get out and open the door for her.

I hurried around the back of the car, wondering what her favorite perversions might be, all the while reminding myself not to get her too drunk. I opened the passenger door, and she brushed up against me as she stepped out. "Come here," she said and gave me a long probing kiss. Then she looked at my front porch and said, "Did you get some packages delivered?"

"What?" I turned and stared at a number of items piled on my front porch just as a head suddenly popped up from behind a grocery bag and barked. "Morton?" I cried and leaped over the front steps, ran up the sidewalk, and took the steps up to the front porch two at a time. "Morton."

He jumped out of the basket placed in front of the door, but his leash had been tied to the door handle, and he couldn't go any further. His golden retriever tail was wagging a mile a minute, slamming into the dog food bags and knocking over the grocery bag full of dog toys.

"Morton, Morton, hey boy, what are you doing here?"

"You have a dog?" AJ asked, walking up the sidewalk behind me.

"No, this is Morton. He belongs to a…to someone I know. I mean used to know. I watched him for a couple of weeks last spring while she went to take care of her mom and dad, some medical thing. She ended up moving down to Atlanta, got a great job offer, and reconnected with some nitwit she knew in high school. God, she took Morton down there with her. He saved my life, actually."

"The dog?"

"Yeah, didn't you, boy? Oh, good boy, good boy. It's so good to see you. Did you miss me, Morton? Did you?" I said, scratching him behind the ears as he licked my face.

"So, ahh, you need some help carrying this stuff inside?"

"What? Oh yeah. Come on in. Let me just get him untied here," I said, undoing the leash from the door. I took my keys out and unlocked the door. Morton pushed with his shoulder just as I began to open the door. "Grab one of those dog food bags there, AJ. Hey, Morton, you remember the place, don't you? We had some good times, didn't we?" I hurried after him as he barged into the entryway, charged through the house into the kitchen, and then ran back out into the living room. He hopped onto the couch, barked a couple of times at a car driving down the street, then followed me as I made my way to the kitchen, turning on the lights as I went.

"I bet you're hungry, aren't you fella? Here how about this," I said, pulling a food dish out of the grocery bag I'd brought in from the porch. Morton barked and hopped back and forth as I set the empty bowl on the floor.

AJ walked into the kitchen and set the dog food bag on the floor, then set her Styrofoam container with the steak on the kitchen counter and started brushing dog food crumbs off the top of her dress. "Oh God, look, I've got dog food all over the front of this new dress."

I couldn't really tell and gave a quick glance as she bounced her breasts up and down. "If you need a paper towel, there's some over by the sink," I said, then went back to scratching Morton behind the ear. AJ seemed to hesitate for a long moment before she strutted over to the sink and tore off a paper towel. I took the dog food bag and filled Morton's food dish. He suddenly looked disappointed.

"Do you have any hand cream?" AJ asked a few minutes later. She was bent over looking in the cabinet under the kitchen sink. As I turned to look at her, she glanced at me over her shoulder and smiled with her perfect bum up in the air. Her tight black dress had risen up an inch or so and just barely exposed the hint of a silky black thong.

I gave her a brief glance, then rubbed Morton some more. "Come on, Morton, you must be starving."

"Hand cream?"

I glanced over at AJ again. She was still bent over only now her entire rear was exposed. The thong ran up her backside to where three little sparkling jewels connected with the waistband. I caught just a glimpse of a lacy tattoo running across the small of her back.

"Oh yeah, it's not down there. It's in that white thing with the push top, right along the back of the sink. Come on, Morton. Don't you like the dog food? You've got to eat. Come on. Here, try this piece."

"So, ahh, any chance on getting that nightcap?"

"What? Sure thing, sorry about that. You can just help yourself. I got hard liquor out in the dining room, help yourself to whatever's in the cabinet with the crystal decanters. White wines are in the fridge, or if you want red, I think there's a bottle in the dining room. It's got a twist-off cap."

"Thanks," she said. In retrospect, I don't think she really meant it.

Morton ignored the dog food in his dish. I tried for a couple of minutes to hand feed it to him, coaxing him one nugget at a time, but he wasn't having any of that action. "Okay, okay, you big baby. But, only because it's your first night, a welcome home treat," I said, then opened the Styrofoam container and placed the remainder of the steak in his dish just as AJ walked back into the kitchen with a glass of dark brown liquid.

"Did you make me one?" I asked.

She glared just as the doorbell rang.

Morton barked and headed toward the front door.

"Who the hell is ringing my doorbell this late at night?"

"It's for me, I called a taxi," she said, took a big sip, shuddered, then set the glass down on the kitchen counter and strutted toward the front door.

"Whoa, AJ. Wait up, wait up," I called and hurried after her.

"It's certainly been memorable. Sorry to interrupt your little boys' reunion. Nice to meet you, Morton," she said.

He hopped off the couch, then shoved his nose in between her legs. She half jumped, then grabbed the back of his head and thrust it back under her skirt. "Oh, God, really cold nose. Well, Dev, I can promise you, he's getting a lot more than you will. Enjoy your night, boys," she said, then slammed the door behind her.

"Hey, hey wait, AJ, AJ," I called. Morton jumped back and forth in front of me, and by the time I got to the door and opened it, the taxi was pulling away from the curb. I watched until the taillights faded up the street, then walked back to the kitchen and dumped the bag with Morton's toys onto the floor. A little handwritten note floated onto the floor.

"Hi, hope all is well. This just isn't working out. Turns out, Buster has an allergy to dogs. I figured you wouldn't mind, besides he likes you, I think. Maddie"

Two

I was sitting in my office chair staring through a set of binoculars, alternating between the working girls waiting for the bus down on the corner and two girls getting dressed in the third-floor apartment across the street. In between times, I was thinking of Morton and then wondering how I could get back into AJ's good graces.

I suppose she was right to be pissed off, but I'd been so happy to see him. I was wondering if I could somehow give her the impression I was really a caring, sensitive guy, and my sensitive side got in the way of taking care of her needs… scratch that. Maybe if I just suggested the caring, sensitive part and—

"Hey, you're in early. I didn't expect to see you until around noon. So how'd the big night go, take any pictures?" Louie asked. He's a pal, my attorney, my office-mate, and half crazy. He tossed his computer bag on his picnic table desk, then emptied what was left in the coffee pot into his giant three-cup mooch mug. "Don't spare any of the details," he said, setting his mug on the edge of my desk then holding his hand out for the binoculars.

"Not much to tell," I said, handing the binoculars over to him.

"Come on, it was the third date. Didn't you take her to that restaurant near your place? I thought you said it was a sure thing? She tell you she was married or something?" He said then proceeded to focus the binoculars on the apartment across the street.

"No, a surprise visitor, actually?"

"What the hell time is it? God, they're already dressed," he groaned and handed back the binoculars.

"Yeah, they must have an early meeting or something, I think they're a good half-hour ahead of their normal schedule."

"Let me guess. It's either a boyfriend or she's into other girls, right? Oh wait, the husband called, right?"

"No, wrong, wrong, and double wrong. Actually, the dinner went great. So great that we skipped dessert, raced to my place, the kisses were coming hot and heavy. We pull up in front of my place, and there he is, on the front porch."

"Who?"

"Morton."

"That dog? The one that knocked up that fancy French poodle show dog?"

"Yeah, Princess Anastasia. He was tied to the front door, along with his bed, a couple of bags of dog food, and his dog toys. Turns out the idiot that Maddie linked up with down in Atlanta has an allergy or something. So she put Morton in the car, drove up here, and left him on my front porch along with a thank-you note."

"You're kidding?"

"No, dead serious. Anyway, AJ got all pissed off, and well, I don't know, maybe she just doesn't like the idea of me having a dog."

"Wait a minute. Didn't you tell me she has a dog, a candy something?"

"A chocolate lab, actually. Yeah, so I'm not really sure why she went off the deep end. I'm getting Morton settled, and the next thing I know, she's heading out the door without so much as a good night kiss. Go figure."

"Doesn't sound like the woman you've described to me. You sure you didn't say something or do…?"

"No, like I said, she just left."

"Strange, so where is Morton?"

"I left him at home, he…"

"Didn't he, you know, chew everything up and trash the place last time you left him there?"

"Yeah, but I'm thinking, he might be a little more mature now. Besides, I've got him confined in the kitchen.

"Wasn't that the room he trashed?"

"Well, yeah, come to think of it." I glanced out the window, the bus had just pulled back into traffic and was heading down the street carrying its lovely cargo toward downtown. The living room light was off in the third-floor apartment across the street, so I tossed the binoculars back on the desk.

"I hope you know what you're doing," Louie said.

"I think they went to work."

"I meant your lady friend. Sounds to me like you screwed up."

"I'll give AJ a call, maybe give her a day or so to calm down first."

"You really want to pursue that? It could end up being a lot of work."

"I think maybe Morton's arrival might have thrown her off course or something. It'll work out. If it doesn't, I'll give Heidi a call."

"That sounds a little more promising," Louie said.

"Heidi's a good friend, but she seems to be able to only take me in little doses."

"You ever think that might have something to do with your lifestyle?"

Three

Over the next couple of days, I left no less than three voicemails for AJ, and she hadn't responded to a single one. So, I phoned Heidi.

"Hey, Heidi, how are things going?"

"I'm not bailing you out if that's why you're calling."

"Why do you always say that? When was the last time I needed bail money?"

"That's not the point. I'm just not doing it anymore, that's all I'm saying."

"Are we crabby today?"

"Why did you call?"

"Are you okay?"

"Yes."

I'd gone this far, so I figured I might as well continue. "Well, it's been a while since I saw you, since we were together. I just thought it might be nice to grab a bite to eat, you know, catch up and…"

"And then you could ply me with wine or margaritas or something, and I'd hop into bed with you. Is that it?"

This wasn't going the way I'd planned. "No, I just wanted to see how you were, make sure everything was okay, that's all. Hey, if you don't want to get together, okay, fine. I just thought it might be nice to see you and…"

"We can meet, but let's not make it your place."

"Okay, should I just bring dinner? I could pick up…"

"No, someplace public. A restaurant might be nice."

I began an internal debate about hanging up.

"Are you still there?" she asked.

"Yes, just trying to think of a restaurant."

"Geno's, I could maybe use some Italian."

"Tonight works for me if you can make it," I said, then hoped she might be busy.

"Say, seven-thirty?" she said.

"Sure. I'll pick you up and…"

"I'll drive myself if it's all the same."

"I'll see you there around seven-thirty. I'll call for a reservation; I know how you hate to wait."

"That would be nice," she said, then hung up.

I didn't know what, but something was wrong. I'd just lined up a dinner date where I'd have the pleasure of dropping a good chunk of change and spending the evening with a very unhappy individual. I could hardly wait.

* * *

True to my word, I made the reservation for seven-thirty, then waited until a little after eight before Heidi finally showed up. I stood as she breezed around the corner. She half-dodged my attempt to give her a kiss, turning her head so I'd plant the kiss on her cheek. Then she pulled away at the last second and sat down while I kissed the air.

"Have you been waiting long?" she said, then stared at the bottle of wine that was now two glasses shy.

"Only since seven-thirty."

"Oh," she said, making it sound like forty minutes wasn't such a bad thing.

"How about some wine?" I said, raising the bottle toward her glass.

"No, none for me."

"No wine?"

"I just told you, no."

"Hey, Heidi, I haven't seen you for at least three weeks. I think we know each other well enough that we can level with one another. So what's going on, what's wrong?"

"Why does something have to be wrong? Just because I don't want a glass of wine doesn't mean…"

"This isn't about the wine. I don't care about that because it just means there's more for me. But your attitude, you were barely civil on the phone this morning. You're almost forty-five minutes late, no text, no phone call—"

"And no dinner date," she said, pushed her chair back, stood, and walked out of the restaurant.

I sat there by myself for ten minutes, hoping she'd come back. She didn't. I was beginning to wonder if it was me? First AJ, now Heidi, who was usually open to just about anything.

"Would you care for an appetizer?" the waiter asked, sounding like he already knew my response. Fittingly, he was dressed for a funeral in a black button-down shirt, black trousers, and a long black apron.

"I think just the check, please."

He reached into a deep apron pocket and handed me the black book with my check already prepared. As he walked away, I pulled a couple of twenties out of my wallet, tossed them on the table, and left.

Four

I'd been leering at the girls in the apartment across the street through my binoculars. The blonde was wearing a black thong and bra, the dark-haired girl just had a white towel wrapped around her. From what I could tell, they both seemed to be talking nonstop while putting on their makeup and sipping coffee at the kitchen counter, multitasking.

"Haskell Investigations," I answered, then picked up the binoculars again.

"Hi, Dev."

"Heidi, hi, how are you doing?"

"I just wanted to apologize for the other night. I didn't mean to walk out. It's just been kind of stressful lately."

"Everything okay?"

"Yeah, I think so. I'm calling because I want to be honest with you. I should have told you the other night, not really sure why I didn't."

"You okay?"

"I've met someone."

Shit. "Heidi, that's great. I'm really happy for you."

"You're not mad?"

I'd tossed the binoculars on my desk, spun around in my chair, and was reaching for a pen. "No, no, I'm very happy for you. Tell me a little about him," I said thinking I'd like to go and smash his car windows.

"Well, we met at a business luncheon. He's an attorney, practices here in town. He helps the handicapped, looks out for their needs."

"Helps the handicapped? Like what, he's a crossing guard on a busy street, or he holds the door open?"

"Very funny. No, he takes legal action on behalf of people with disabilities. You know, making sure buildings, retail shops, and things like that are in compliance with the law."

"Wow, an upstanding guy. Sounds like I probably don't have a chance. What's his name?"

"Austin, Austin Hackett. He's originally from Chicago, but he's been practicing up here for fourteen or fifteen years."

"Interesting," I said, writing down the bastard's name on a bar coaster advertising Two Hearted Ale. "What firm is he with?"

"He has a private practice. Say, you're not thinking of poking around and making his life miserable, are you? That's not why I called. If you think…"

"Hey, calm down. I'm not going to poke around, as you say. I was just curious. I know a lot of legal beagles in a number of different firms. I thought I might have run into him before, that's all."

"I don't think he spends much time in the kind of places you go, Dev. No offense, but, well, he doesn't mingle with criminals."

"Good for him," I said. "So, how long have you been seeing each other?" The last time I'd spent the night with Heidi had been over a month ago.

"Oh, we've been together for a good three weeks," she said, making it sound like it had been three years. If memory served, Heidi's relationships usually tanked right around week four. I reached over for my desk calendar, flipped the pages seven days ahead, then penned her name in and added a question mark behind it.

"Heidi, I'm really happy for you. I'd love to meet him sometime," I lied.

"You know, that might not be such a good idea."

"Oh?"

"Well, we wanted to be completely honest with one another, and one night we just, you know, told each other about all our past relationships and things."

I couldn't believe Heidi told this guy about all her past relationships. There wasn't enough time in the day. Three weeks? God, she'd still be unloading. She must have skipped an awful lot.

"What about him?"

"Actually, I'm his first. He was always so busy. He took care of his sick parents. Then, once they passed away, he became a Navy Seal. He went to law school, and when he graduated at the top of his class, he decided to dedicate himself to helping others in honor of his parents."

Heidi is one of, if not *the* sharpest businesswoman I know. She's made enough money to never really have to worry about money anymore. That said, if she's got a weak spot, it has to do with romantic interests feeding her a line. The bigger the line, the more readily she seems to believe it.

"Wow, he sounds like a really great guy. No wonder you fell in love with him, and he'd be crazy not to go after you." The jerk. "How 'bout we get together, a celebration in honor of you two finding one another?"

"You're not mad?"

"Well, I'd love it if he hadn't found you, but I'm happy for you, Heidi. Really, I am. You pick the place, and I'll pay for dinner."

"You're sure? You don't have to, you know."

"Yeah, I know."

"And I'm not going to bed with you, Dev. I just want to have dinner, and then we'll go our separate ways at the end, okay?"

"Yeah, I get it, believe me. Just a little celebration. I'm really happy for you, honey, honest."

"Okay, let me think of a place, and I'll just send you a text. What night works for you?"

"You name the night, and I'll cancel whatever I have going." The only thing I had on my calendar was a note that The Spot bar was doing two for one night on Thursday.

"You're sweet. Thanks for not being all mad and going crazy."

"Heidi, you've just become the one who got away. It's my loss, but I'm really happy for you."

Five

Louie stepped into the office just as I slammed down the phone.

"Whoa, take it easy. You'll break that thing into a hundred different pieces. Someone coming after you with a paternity suit?"

"No. God, the way things are going, there's no chance of that happening in the foreseeable future. Hey, you ever hear of a guy practicing named Austin Hackett? I guess he does disability work."

"That prick? Is he jacking around someone you know?"

"Yeah, but not legally. At least I don't think so."

Louie grabbed his coffee mug and headed toward the pot as he spoke. "Austin Hackett. He's got a private practice, works a scam on small to medium business folks. He has at least a couple of guys that I know of. I think he keeps them on retainer. One's sight-impaired, the other's missing a leg. They fake an injury at some small business. You know maybe trip on a step, fall in the bathroom or out on the sidewalk, stuff like that. Then Hackett sues on behalf of his 'clients' and scams the business into settling out of court."

"At what point does the system wise up? It sounds like it could be grounds for disbarment."

"It probably could, if it ever goes to court. What Hackett does is he comes up with a laundry list of potential problems, entries, exits, elevators, handicap access to the restroom, all sorts of shit. By the time he's finished the bill to fix all that usually starts around six figures and climbs. A lot of little places just can't afford that. So, being the good guy, Austin Hackett offers to settle for, oh five, six maybe ten grand, depending, and the cases never go to court."

"And that's legal?"

"Technically, yeah. I think the state has looked into him a couple of times. Not sure about the bar association, but like I said, it's legal."

"Sounds like a scam."

"Oh, absolutely. Go on the low side, say he settles for just fifty percent. Fifty percent of five grand is twenty-five hundred. Pay your handicapped guy two hundred, and basically, Hackett is netting something like two grand or more a day, every day. Nice work if you can get it."

"And he's getting away with this?"

"He seems to be, at least thus far. Google him, he's within the letter of the law. He suing someone you know?"

"Not suing. It's Heidi, she's seeing him. From the sound of things, she's fallen head over heels for the bastard. Thinks he's the greatest thing since sliced bread. Navy Seal, took care of his dying parents…"

"Who told you that shit?"

"Heidi. I just got off the phone with her. We're going to have a farewell dinner."

"She's not marrying Hackett, is she?"

"Only because he hasn't asked. According to her, they've been seeing one another for three weeks now."

"Get her away from him, Dev. He'll find a way to take her for every cent she's got, then just cast her aside. Oh, and Navy Seal? I'm pretty sure he couldn't swim from here to the door and back. Navy Seal? Jesus," he said and just shook his head.

Six

I put the binoculars back in my desk drawer, left the girls in the apartment to their own devices, and started looking into Austin Hackett online. There were almost three pages' worth of links, all pretty much the same, just like Louie had described. The newspaper seemed to tout him as a crusader. He'd been sued twice and lost both cases. I made note of the people who filed the complaints. I'd want to talk with them and, hopefully, their attorneys.

Toward the bottom of page three, two links mentioned a lawsuit filed on behalf of a wounded veteran, one Marcel Barker. If it was the Marcel Barker I knew, he was indeed a wounded veteran, but his 'wound' had occurred at the hands of a disgruntled husband returning home two days early to Portsmouth Naval Shipyard from some test cruise back in the early seventies. Marcel, I knew him as "Woofy," was a guard at the Portsmouth Naval Prison up until the time he was shot in the ass by that returning husband. There were political connections somewhere along the way, and Woofy was discharged and placed on disability. To my knowledge, the husband never served any time. In fact, I don't think the case ever went to court.

I hadn't seen Woofy in a number of years, but I had a pretty good idea of the half dozen different places I might be able to find him.

"I gotta check out some stuff. Lock up if you leave," I said to Louie.

"I'm in court at eleven, pleading a no contest. You want me to ask around about your pal Hackett?"

"You mind?"

"No, I've never liked the guy. Along with most other practicing attorneys, I would love to see him get nailed with something, anything."

"Yeah, see what you can find out. I'd appreciate that," I said, then headed out the door to find Woofy.

I asked about him at Wangs, the Yuk Club, the Poodle, and Ugly's. They'd all seen him recently but didn't know where he was at the moment. I was running out of options when I found him at the fifth place I checked, the Manhole.

The Manhole isn't that far removed from its name. Not a lot of people go there for a variety of reasons. But the few who do enter are well looked after because they're there to do business, and the business is drinking.

It's a dark, dismal little place on a crusty side street in a back corner just off the downtown railway yard. The front door had a handle that I think was supposed to be brass, at least at one time, but it was so crusted with grime you couldn't really tell. The door itself had a window, four inches wide and maybe five feet long running from the top to the bottom, and had been boarded over with a sheet of weathered plywood for as long as I could remember. The story I heard was there had been a shooting back in the late '80s. Fortunately, the shooter was too drunk to hit anything other than the window.

It was the middle of the afternoon on a pleasant, sunny day when I entered the place. None of the dozen people in there bothered to look up as I stepped inside and let my eyes adjust to the inky darkness. As my vision began to return, I could make out a number of folks sitting alone at the bar. It seemed they'd all made a point of positioning themselves at least two stools apart so they could focus on the task at hand, drinking, and not be interrupted. Two women occupied a back booth and seemed to be the only people engaged in any social interaction.

"What'll I get you?" the bartender said and smeared whatever had spilled on the bar with a rag that looked like it had been used to clean the floor in the men's room.

"I'm looking for someone, and I wondered if—"

"They ain't here," he said, tossed the bar rag back on the floor, and walked down to the far end of the bar.

"Kenny's a real asshole, ain't he?" the guy sitting a couple of stools away said. He shrugged his shoulders like he was laughing to himself and didn't bother to look at me.

"Yeah, and that's probably his good side. Can I buy you another?"

"Never turned one down," he said then raised his glass to catch the bartender's attention. "Who you looking for?"

"Woofy Barker, you know him?"

"Yeah, everybody knows, Woofy. What's he done this time?"

"Surprisingly, nothing. I just wanted to ask him about a guy."

"You a cop?"

"Me? No, I'm trying to find a guy Woofy knew a while back. Thought he might be able to help is all."

The guy nodded but didn't say anything else. His drink arrived a moment later, "Three seventy-five," Kenny said, looking at me and trying to sound friendly. I wondered how he knew I was paying then figured the guy I was chatting with probably came in every afternoon and nursed the same drink for three or four hours.

I handed a five-dollar bill over.

"You want change?" He sounded hopeful.

"Yes."

He tossed the change on the bar a moment later, the quarter rolled off the bar, but I managed to catch it before it hit the floor. He glanced longingly at the dollar bill floating in the beer puddle on the bar, then frowned and wandered back down to the far end. Once he left, my guy drained his glass, then pulled the fresh drink in a little closer.

"So you're looking for Woofy. You sure he's not in any trouble?"

"Well, from what I know of Woofy, yes, he probably is in trouble, but not with me. I just wanted to ask him some questions is all."

"And you're not a cop?"

"Nope, actually just trying to find something out about another guy."

He seemed to think about that for a sip or two, then said, "You want Woofy, he's catching a little nap back in that corner booth."

I looked across the dark room toward the corner booth. Sure enough, a pair of feet were just barely hanging out of the booth. Three or four empty glasses littered the table.

"You said the bartender's name was Kenny."

"Yeah, and I also said he was an asshole."

"No disagreement from me." I signaled Kenny with half a wave. He took his time, finished the conversation he was involved in, then slowly made his way back down to me. He glanced at the dollar bill, still floating in the puddle, more wet than dry.

"Yeah."

"Just a cup of coffee, keep the change," I said then laid another five on the bar.

Seven

Kenny poured steaming coffee into a white ceramic mug. The coffee was so hot you'd swear it was going to burn the glaze off the mug. I could smell the stuff from across the bar, burnt coffee. It had probably been on the burner for the past forty-eight hours, guaranteed to give you heartburn. But then, who drank coffee in this place?

I carried the mug back toward the feet hanging out of the corner booth. I picked up my pace as I headed across the room because the mug seemed to be getting hotter, and it was beginning to burn my hand. I set the mug down on the table, then kicked the pair of feet a few times until I started to get a reaction.

"Humph, argh, cough, groan, cough, cough."

The two women sitting a couple of booths away were suddenly quiet for a few seconds before they started up again. "I sure hope that isn't contagious," one of them said.

"Hey, Woofy old pal, good to see you. Come on, wake up. Look, I bought you a drink." That seemed to get things moving, and the figure slouched in the booth suddenly began to move and pull himself upright. He squinted across the table at the empty glasses trying to get his bearings.

"What the hell, is that coffee?" he said, then peered up at me with an uncomprehending look.

"Just to get started. Once you're awake, we'll see what you need."

That provided some added incentive, and he reached out with a shaky hand and slowly pulled the mug toward him. He sniffed and blew on the mug a half dozen times, slurped a little, and made a face. "Oh God, that shit's really bad."

I was pretty sure I couldn't argue the point. I waited while he sipped some more then said, "So Woofy, you happen to know a guy named Austin Hackett."

"That asshole?" he said then blew on the mug a few more times before he slurped again. "Argh, this is really bad."

"What can you tell me about Hackett?"

"You some kind of a cop?"

"Nope, I'm the guy who's buying you a drink once you finish that coffee. I just want to find out anything you can tell me about Austin Hackett."

"Well, he made me a sweetheart deal, then when it come time to pay up, he didn't. Simple as that."

"What was the deal?"

"Nothing fancy. I went into this doctor's office. I think he was one of them chiropractors. Anyway, I go in there, see about making an appointment. Course I didn't, then on the way out," he glanced toward the bar, I guess checking to see if anyone was listening then lowered his voice. "On the way out, I fake a fall, see? He's waiting down on the corner, Hackett is, and he calls 911 for the paramedics. Couple of days later, he threatens to sue this doctor. He's got all sorts of these trumped-up charges that'll run 'em over a hundred grand. Then, he offered to settle for I think it was eight grand." He took another slurp then cringed as the coffee burned its way down to his stomach. "God, but this is bad."

"And what did you get out of it?"

"Well, first of all, I'm a disabled veteran," he said and sat up just a little straighter in the booth.

"Yeah, well look, about that, Woofy. I think you were shot in the ass by a disgruntled husband if I recall, but they gave you the disability anyway."

"Oh, so you know about that, do ya?"

I nodded. "I don't really care about any of that. Did this Hackett make it worth your while?"

"Hell, no," he half-shouted. "Bastard was supposed to split the money with me. Ended up giving me a couple hundred bucks cash, and told me if I complained he'd have someone put me in the hospital for real."

"What did you do?"

Woofy looked at me like I was crazy and said, "Well, I took the money, of course. I didn't like what he done, but then again, it was cash."

"Anyone from that doctor's office ever contact you?"

"There was some meeting that was gonna be set up, me being dispossessed."

"You mean, deposed?"

"Yeah, that's it. But Hackett told me not to worry. Said things would never get that far. Next thing I know, he's telling me it's all over, and all he could give me was two hundred."

"You do anything else for the guy?"

"No, never heard from him again, which is just fine by me. I been screwed around enough in life. I don't need to go looking for someone to do it."

"What are you drinking?"

"You buying?"

I nodded, then said, "Tell you what, here's twenty bucks, get whatever you want. I appreciate the help."

"Anytime, man, anytime," he said as he snatched up the twenty I'd just tossed on the table and slid out of the booth.

Eight

I was thinking about what Louie had said, reminding me how Morton destroyed the kitchen the last time I left him alone in there. So, after I left the Manhole, I drove to my place. Morton hadn't trashed the kitchen, but only because he'd somehow gotten out of the kitchen and trashed the entire house. He'd carried a feather pillow down from my bedroom upstairs, then apparently ran through the house with the thing leaving a trail of feathers all over the first floor.

He'd gotten hold of the coffee cake I'd planned on serving AJ and devoured that, breaking the plate it was sitting on and knocking over a kitchen stool in the process. He chewed two of the legs on the kitchen stool. He found his way into my pantry cabinet and dragged one of the dog food bags through the first-floor scattering dog food among all the pillow feathers.

It must have taken quite an effort because when I got home, he was asleep on the living room couch with feathers hanging from his nose. I just closed my eyes and hoped it would all go away. It didn't.

* * *

Morton barked and ran over to the door when Louie came back to the office.

"I thought you said he was at home, in the kitchen or something," Louie said, then bent down and gave Morton a good rub behind the ears.

"He was. I just got to thinking maybe he shouldn't be there the entire day by himself, so I thought I'd bring him down here for a bit. You okay with that?"

"Not a problem. What the hell is this? A feather?" Louie said then pulled a small white feather from Morton's tail.

"Wow, I wonder where he got that?"

"Yeah," Louie said, sounding suspicious, but he didn't go any further.

Fortunately, my phone rang. "Haskell Investigations."

"Hi, Dev, it's AJ, I'm returning your call."

"Calls," I said and waited.

"Well?"

"Look, I'm sorry if I upset you, I…"

"Upset me? Oh no, Dev, you didn't upset me. You couldn't be bothered. As a matter of fact, you completely ignored me."

I put on my knee pads and began to grovel. "Look, you're right, and I was wrong, very wrong. I was just so caught off guard when I found Morton on the front porch. I didn't know how to handle it. I guess I didn't realize how important he was to me. Did I mention he saved my life?"

"Actually, you did, I think a couple of times."

"Oh, well look, I'm sorry if I upset you, but I just got caught off guard, blindsided. I had a wonderful time with you, and well, I was hoping I could maybe see you again."

"Hmm-mmm."

"Oh yeah, and I'm sorry, too. Really I am." I saw the look in Louie's eye, but I didn't care.

"Thanks, that was sweet, I think. It's not that I don't like dogs. I do, I told you about Lady Godiva."

"Who?"

"Dev, Lady Godiva, my chocolate lab. She'll be three this fall. I just love her."

"Yeah, you did tell me. I've just been so focused on you. I guess I wasn't paying attention."

Louie rolled his eyes.

"Hmm-mmm, okay, forgiven as long as it doesn't happen again."

"Yeah, you're right. So, I was wondering if maybe you'd consider getting together sometime if that would be okay. I promise not to get distracted, believe me."

"I'd like that. I tell you what. You know that coffee shop just down the street from you?"

"You mean, Nina's?"

"Yeah, why don't you and Morton meet Lady Godiva and me for a cup of coffee tonight, say half-past-seven? They can get to know one another, and well, we can get reacquainted, too."

"Tonight, half-past-seven. I'd like that."

"So would I."

"Okay, we'll see you there."

"Good, and Dev, thanks for the phone messages and for the apology. It means a lot to me."

"Thanks for returning my calls, AJ."

"Bye, bye, bye," she said and hung up.

It felt like a weight I didn't even know was there had suddenly been lifted.

"Sounded like your groveling did the trick," Louie said without looking up from his laptop.

"I make no bones about it. I can grovel with the best of them. The only thing I care about is that it seemed to work. Come on, Morton. Let's head home and get that mess cleaned up. We just might be having sleepover company tonight."

Nine

orton and I were at the coffee shop fifteen minutes early. I tied him up to the wrought-iron railing out front, then went inside and grabbed a coffee. I described AJ and told Jimmy, the barista I'd pay for her coffee and anything else she wanted.

I watched AJ approach with Lady Godiva about twenty minutes later. Godiva was lean, sleek, and appeared to be very well trained. AJ was wearing a pair of skin-tight shorts and a top with spaghetti straps and a plunging neckline. When they stopped on the corner and waited for a car to pass, Lady Godiva immediately sat. Then they stepped off, and the dog kept perfect pace as they crossed the street. A guy driving past tooted his horn a couple of times, but AJ ignored him.

She greeted Morton outside with a big rub under his chin, then she attached Lady Godiva's leash to the wrought-iron railing right next to Morton's and came inside. A couple of heads turned as she waved at me and signaled she was going to order a coffee.

"Oh, that was sweet of you," she said, giving me a little peck on the cheek as she sat down. "You didn't have to buy me coffee." She placed her mug on the table, some frothy thing, Jimmy had made a design in the shape of a heart floating on the top.

"I thought it was the least I could do. Would you like a pastry or anything? They've got a great apple tart."

"I'd love one, but it will go right to my hips, so I'll just take a pass. Well," she said and took a sip. "How have you been?"

"I just want to say in person how very sorry I am about the other night, I…"

"Dev, it's okay, we all make mistakes. I'm hoping we can just move on."

"I'd like that."

"So, tell me what you've been up to," she said, then took a sip from her mug and sexily ran her tongue over her upper lip. "Mmm-mmm."

"Well, I just took on a new case, looking into someone trying to work an angle on people with disabilities. I…"

"What? God, some people can be so low. Can you imagine? I hope you get him. Jail would be too good. Who in their right mind…" She went on for the next ten minutes about how awful people could be. I might have added to her rant a little by telling her I was doing the case pro bono, that I just wanted to set things right. I didn't mention Austin Hackett by name and only slightly embellished certain aspects. Naturally, I didn't mention Heidi.

"You really are a sweet guy, Dev," she said once she'd finished her rant. Then she slid her chair over, reached beneath the table, ran her hand back and forth along the side of my leg a few times, and smiled. "I'm glad we're talking again, I really missed you," she said.

There was laughing from the front of the room, and about a half dozen people were standing and staring out the window. One guy started clapping, and some woman yelled, "Oh my God." I was curious but didn't want to interrupt the AJ action under the table.

The couple at the table next to us got up and moved to the front window to see what the commotion was all about. AJ gave a subtle look around and then moved her hand onto the top of my thigh, tickling with her fingers, moving a little closer with every rub to where I hoped she'd end up.

She smiled and stared into my eyes. I could tell her breathing was as heavy as mine. "I've wanted you ever since the first time I laid eyes on you," she said, then started to rub her nails along the inside of my thigh as her eyes flared. "Do you think you have enough dog food for two dogs at breakfast?"

"If I don't, I can always go get some. I'd like to do an up-close study of that little tattoo you have."

"I've been counting on it. Shall we continue this at your place?"

Two women shrieked in the crowd up by the front window. Now there were at least a dozen people crowded around looking at something and laughing. Virtually everyone in the place, except AJ and I, stood at the window. Jimmy, the barista, was hurrying our way.

The same woman screamed again, "Oh my God!"

"Hey, Dev, we've got a bit of a situation out front. Is that your dog looks like a golden retriever?"

"Morton, yeah, why? What's he doing?" I asked.

AJ said a worried sounding, "Lady Godiva," removed her hand from inside my thigh and hurried toward the door. I was right behind her. A number of heads in the crowd turned as we stepped outside.

One guy called, "Thanks for the show."

Some old bat yelled, "Absolutely disgusting."

AJ gave a short scream and yelled, "Morton, get off her. Dev, do something. Oh my God."

I stepped out to see Morton mounted on Lady Godiva. A city bus was stopped on the corner. The driver had opened the door and just sat there staring and smiling as Morton rode Lady Godiva for all he was worth. For her part, the Lady seemed to be giving as good as she got, letting out deep groans that suggested she just might be enjoying herself. All of the passengers on the bus were looking out the window, pointing and laughing. A couple of cellphone cameras flashed.

"God, Dev do something, do something," AJ shouted. Her mood had definitely changed from just a moment ago.

"Morton, damn it, come on, get off, get off," I said, undoing his leash and gently tugging.

Morton gave me a look that suggested, "You've got to be kidding."

"Come on, Morton, come on," I said, coaxing him off Lady Godiva.

AJ had untied Lady Godiva's leash from the wrought-iron railing and was encouraging her in the opposite direction. Gradually we broke their embrace. Clapping and cheers erupted from inside the coffee shop and on the bus as folks slowly returned to their normal activities. Some guy in the coffee shop took a cellphone picture of AJ.

"God, what is wrong with you two?" she said, glaring first at Morton and then at me. Her face was red, and she wasn't looking all that happy— more like she wanted to kill. Fortunately, the bus pulled away. We could both hear the scattered applause as it headed down the street.

"I don't know what to tell you. He's never done anything like that before. Is your dog in heat?" I didn't feel the need to tell her about Morton impregnating Princess Anastasia at the dog show last spring.

"God," she screamed, red-faced, just as a cellphone camera flashed from inside the coffee shop again. I glared at the guy, and he gave a little wave before returning to his table.

"Come on, let's head over to my place, and maybe things will look a little better after…"

"Your place? Are you crazy? After this?" She half screamed, then yanked on Lady Godiva's leash and took off down the street.

"Hey, AJ, AJ," I called, but they kept on moving and didn't look back. Some guy drove past and whistled out the window at the two of them. AJ gave him the finger and shouted something I couldn't quite make out.

Morton gave off a little whine as we watched them depart.

"Don't even start, you."

Ten

My luck seemed to be running about the same the following morning. The girls in the apartment were nowhere to be seen, and it was raining out, so all the women at the bus stop were clad in raincoats and hovered under umbrellas. Morton was busy, ensconced in his bed in front of the filing cabinet, and working on an old chew toy I'd found in the back of a desk drawer. I was online reviewing the Austin Hackett links and not really coming up with anything new when Louie came in.

He was wearing what was probably a wrinkled navy blue pinstripe suit except that he was dripping wet, and so a lot of the wrinkles had disappeared along with any crease left in his trousers. "Man, it's pouring out there. I'm soaked to the bone. The apartment girls sleeping in?"

"I think they may have left early. You know, maybe you should hang that coat up so it can dry, at least a little."

"Good idea," he said, then peeled off his coat and hung it on one of the pegs next to the door. His shoulders and halfway down the back of his shirt were soaked as well. Water dripped off the ends of his suit coat sleeves.

"Actually, I wonder if it wouldn't work better if you put that suit coat on a hanger." I gave a nod toward a wooden hanger dangling from the file cabinet, where Morton was busily chewing.

"Oh yeah, sure," he said, then draped his coat haphazardly over the hanger and hooked it on the handle of the file drawer. He bent down and gave Morton a good rub, then drained the coffee pot into his mooch mug. "Okay, don't spare any details. Tell me about your date. Hopefully, someone around here got some action last night."

"Oh, someone did, it just wasn't me."

"Well, don't look at me. I'd be the last guy. You said it was a sure thing. What the hell happened?" Louie asked, then grimaced after taking a swallow of coffee.

"Morton."

"She's into…"

"No, not that." I proceeded to tell Louie the tale. I maybe doubled the size of the crowd, might have mentioned a few more people taking pictures, but the basic facts remained the same.

"God, Morton," Louie laughed. "I don't know if I should give you congratulations or a warning."

"It was really going my way, too. I've already phoned AJ with what's becoming my standard apology."

"What did she say?"

"She didn't. I just got dumped into her voice mail."

"I don't know, Dev. Maybe this one just wasn't meant to be."

"Man, and we were so close. We were literally go-ing to head over to my place, and she was going to spend the night. But idiot over there had other ideas." I nodded in Morton's direction. "He could have had action all night long, but no, he thought it would be more fun to please a crowd." My computer made a ding sound sig-naling a Facebook message.

"Think she'll phone you back?"

"I'd say there's probably less than a fifty-fifty chance. The little I know, it seems she's pretty protective of her dog. I mean, I guess I really can't blame her for being pissed off. But on the other hand, if the thing was in heat, why would you tie her up in front of a building on a busy street corner? That's just asking for trouble, especially since it was her idea for the dogs to meet and get to know each other. Of course, Morton being Mor-ton…"

Morton looked up at me with his tongue hanging out.

"Well, at least someone got some action. He's ap-parently doing better than you or me," Louie said

I clicked into my Facebook account, then clicked on messages. "Don't go taking his side, Louie. He— Oh shit."

"Problem?"

Terry Davis was a guy I knew barely well enough to say hi to. I remembered seeing him at Nina's last night, although we'd just exchanged nods. His Facebook mes-sage read, "Thanks for the show last night." He'd posted an image of me tugging on Morton's leash while he rode Lady Godiva. Terry had tagged me in the image. Fortunately, he didn't mention AJ. "She's gonna kill me."

"Can you delete it?"

"Yeah, first, I better remove my name." I clicked on the Facebook edit and removed my name, then deleted the image from my site. I sent Terry a message explaining the situation and asking him to delete the image. "Damn Internet," I groaned.

"Look at it this way, Morton is now world-famous."

"I'm not sure that really helps."

"Hey, I did some checking yesterday after my court appearance. Asked around about your pal, Austin Hackett. Got some names for you," Louie said, then opened his computer bag and took out a couple of bar napkins. One was from the Black Dog pub with two names written on it, and the other, from the Gopher Bar, had three names written down.

"You can check both those guys on the Black Dog napkin. They've gone up against Hackett in court and won, I might add. He may be a jerk. He is, in fact, but he seems to have this thing wired, and the battles he's lost in the courtroom, only made him adjust tactics and go for a settlement out of court. Just in chatting with folks, I think you'd have to go a way before you heard anything nice about him. I sure didn't pick anything up."

"And these three names you got at the Gopher Bar?" I held up the napkin.

"Those are his ex-wives."

"He's got three?"

"Yeah, I thought you might find that interesting."

"Heidi thinks he's never been married."

"Yeah, well, just add that to the laundry list. Didn't he tell her he was a Navy Seal, too? Like I said before, I'm pretty sure he can't even swim."

"He told her he was from Chicago. Said he took care of his sick parents until they died, then went into the service."

"Gee, imagine? Probably an altar boy, too. I wonder where he ever found the time to fit three wives in?"

"You find anything out about these women?"

"Just the names and the guy I talked to said those were their maiden names, so they may have reverted back to that. They may still go by Hackett, or maybe they remarried and are going by a new name."

"All in Ramsey County?"

"That I don't know. You gonna call Heidi?"

"God, I'd love to, but I'm going to need some backup proof. She sounded really smitten with this jerk. She never believes anything I tell her unless I can back it up, and even then, it's going to be tough to convince her."

"Which reminds me," Louie said.

"What's that?"

"He's supposed to be a real control freak."

Eleven

Nowadays, the phonebook is virtually useless unless you're looking for someone over sixty-five years of age. I went online, clicked onto the white pages' site, and began checking the ex-wives' names. Connie Adams was the first name. There were nine possibles listed on the site between Constance and Connie. Three more if you spelled the last name with two d's, Addams. Those were just the names for St. Paul; there were a dozen more in Minneapolis. Of the twenty-four potentials, only two answered their phone. One said she didn't know anyone by the name of Austin Hackett. The other woman hung up, which didn't eliminate her as a potential ex-wife. In fact, to a certain way of thinking, it may have moved her up to the top of the list. Twenty-four potential names, and that was just the first of three individuals. There had to be an easier way.

I called a guy I knew.

"Ramsey County Records."

"Ray McCormick, please."

"One moment."

After three rings, he answered, "Ray McCormick."

"Ray, long time, Dev Haskell."

There was a slight pause, and the tone sounded decidedly cooler. "Hello, Dev. Been at least a couple of years. Lucky me. What's this about?"

"I was wondering if you could look up a couple-three names for me, I need some phone numbers and—"

"Well, aside from violating local, state, and federal statutes, I still can't do that. If you're looking for a phone number, you might think about going online or, God forbid, the phonebook."

"That's why I'm calling you, Ray. I've tried both and just ran around in circles. Listen, you got half a minute so I can explain my situation?"

"I'll do better than that, Dev. I'll give you a full sixty seconds before I hang up."

"Okay, I'm doing some background investigation for the state bar," I lied. "They've got an attorney scamming disabled people. I'm trying to contact his former wives. He's got three. I'm not sure if the women are even in St. Paul, let alone Ramsey County. But I was thinking, if you could check county divorce records, you know just a cross-reference on this guy's last name, maybe something might come up. I'm really dangling at the end of my rope here."

There was a long pause before he spoke. "What's his name?"

"Hackett, Austin Hackett," I said, and spelled out the last name for Ray.

"That maybe rings a bell. What's his scam?" he asked, I could hear him clicking a keyboard in the background.

"It sounds above board. He goes after buildings and retailers that aren't up with the ADA, Americans with Disabilities Act. He has handicapped people scout the place out, promises them a few grand for their trouble, but then the case never goes any further. He always settles out of court for something in the neighborhood of six to ten grand, basically legal blackmail. Then he gives the handicapped person maybe a hundred bucks and tells them to get screwed."

"One of the news stations do something on this guy awhile back?"

I happened to have watched the hundred and twenty-second piece online just the night before. "Yeah, as a matter of fact, channel eleven if I'm not mistaken, he—"

"You got a pen there?"

"I do, fire away."

"I've got a Nancette Reilly," he spelled both names out for me. "That was in December of twenty-fourteen. You said you had three names?"

"Yeah."

"I'm only finding the one divorce in Ramsey county. Maybe the other two were in another county or hell, maybe even out of state. Here's the address on the Reilly woman, well at least the address we have. But it wouldn't be too unusual if she's moved since this was filed."

"Can't thank you enough, Ray. This really helps."

"I'll tell you how you can thank me, Dev. These are a matter of public record. You pay a small fee, and you can get the info, so please don't call me again. Good luck, nice chatting," he said and hung up.

I went back to the white pages' site, armed with the address and the correct spelling I found the woman I was looking for and placed the phone call. I got dumped into a voicemail and left a message. My phone rang about a half-hour later.

"Haskell Investigations."

"Devlin Haskell, please, I'm returning a phone call he left for me." She spoke softly, and there was the hint of a regional accent, although I couldn't place from where.

"Is this Nancette?"

"Yes." She half laughed and said, "I prefer Nancy."

"Nancy, I'm a private investigator. I'm working on a case looking into the dealings an individual named Austin Hackett has had with a number of handicapped individuals."

"Has he hired you?" she asked, making it sound more like an accusation than a simple question.

"No, to be honest, at this stage, I don't believe he's even aware I'm looking into the situation. I can state for a fact he has not, and certainly will not be hiring me."

"So, you're going after him?"

"I suppose that would be an accurate statement."
"We should meet," she said.

Twelve

ancy Reilly was an attractive red-headed woman with an aura of someone who knew her way around. She reminded me an awful lot of Heidi. I was seated at the bar in Kincaid's and waved. She was the only redhead looking around once she'd stepped in the door. She nodded the moment I caught her attention and headed in my direction.

"Nancy? Hi, I'm Dev Haskell. Thanks for taking the time to meet with me. Can I get you something?"

"Vodka martini, dirty," she said to the bartender who'd watched her crossing the room and just happened to wash up on shore at the same time she did.

"Tough workday?" I asked

"No, I just came from my therapist. I always seem to need a little fortification after one of those sessions."

"I hope everything's okay."

"What? Oh yeah, thanks, but no worries. It's not like I'm going to go up into some tower and start screaming. Well, I'd love to scream at one person." She raised her eyebrows and smiled. "It was part of my divorce settlement. Since Austin has to pay for the sessions as long as

I need them, I guess I'll just plan on *needing* them for a very long time."

"You were divorced in December of twenty-fourteen?"

"Yeah, officially, but I'd moved out months before that, lived with a number of different friends."

"Tough getting resettled, I suppose."

"No, not really. I was glad to get away from him. God, was I glad. But I'm not sure how much you know about Austin. He can be difficult. He was actually stalking me in the end, and at one point, I feared for my life."

"What did he do?"

"He'd park outside my condo every night. He came to my office a couple of times until my boss threatened to beat him up. He followed me, contacted people we knew, and told them lies. According to him, I was using drugs, was mentally ill, had a drinking problem, a secret lover, had drained his bank accounts, was infected with HIV, the list goes on and on. I filed a restraining order, which slowed him down a little. Then I got a conceal and carry permit, and that seemed to put a stop to his antics. In the end, he didn't contest the divorce. We settled the financial aspects, and with the exception of my therapist and an annual trip to Paris, he has no other financial obligations."

"An annual trip to Paris?"

"Two of the lies he spread about me were that I was crazy and that I had a lover in Paris. So, as long as that was the case," she laughed. "I figured he could just pay for the privilege. I like to think of it as just a helpful little reminder to keep his big fat mouth shut. Anyway, you're investigating his American's with Disabilities lawsuits?"

I thought for a moment and debated about coming clean. "Actually, no. At least not in so many words. Here's what I'm doing," I said then went on to explain Heidi's situation, my concerns, and my need to have accurate and strong information backing me up before I said anything to her.

"I wish I'd had a friend like you when he was sweeping me off my feet. How long has she been seeing him?"

"She told me its been about three weeks. I'm guessing it's been a little longer than that."

She nodded, then said, "He likes to strike while the iron's hot. I'd guess there's probably a diamond ring in her not too distant future."

"A diamond ring?"

"Cubic zirconium, actually," she laughed. "He'll give her a set of falsified insurance papers for safekeeping, so she won't get it evaluated. The papers will list the value at ten, or maybe he's moved it up a notch, and now it's closer to fifteen thousand."

"You're kidding?"

"Nope. He'll do some overly flamboyant thing, like take her on a romantic getaway. He took me to Paris for three days and popped the question beneath the Eiffel Tower. I mean right beneath it. Got down on his knees, had the ring in a box from Tiffany's if you can believe it. God only knows where he got the box. All sorts of tourists were taking cellphone pictures of us. God, I must be on half the cellphones in China and Japan," she laughed.

"We were married a week later by some guy who got his license in a drug store or something. Austin moved in with me, said it would just be until he closed some big, complicated, stock transaction. Next thing I know, everything started going downhill. I think he really likes the romancing part, and to be honest, I loved it. Flowers sent to my office every three or four days, little gifts, running with the "in" crowd. Hey, I'm a farm girl from southern Iowa. Most of the girls I went to high school with never made it to college. They're working twenty-four-seven on a two-hundred-acre farm where they'll never make any money, or they're a waitress at a twenty-four-hour truck stop somewhere on the Interstate. Sound anything like your friend?" she asked, then took the first sip from her drink.

"No, not really, and I guess that's the surprising thing. She's not stupid, I mean not that you're stupid. Actually, now that I think about it, the two of you seem to be very similar. Educated, successful in your field, hard-working. She's one sharp lady."

She nodded, smiled, and said, "And her clock is ticking."

I must have given a funny look, signaling I wasn't following.

"The biological clock. Whether she admits it or not, at least part of the time, she's thinking about settling down. She probably has times when she lowers her standards," Nancy nodded toward me. "And, of course, that never seems to work. Then, out of nowhere comes this successful, decent looking guy who just sweeps you off your feet. God," she said, and suddenly got this far away look in her eyes.

"You just want to eat him alive. Well, actually, I pretty much did. All your friends are happy for you. It's a whirlwind, and of course, you know he's the one, because, well, you're you and you didn't make a mistake, and you didn't lower your standards and besides, look at all the gifts. Then one morning you wake up, and suddenly you didn't set the table quite right, the silverware isn't straight, his three-minute egg took three minutes and ten seconds. Even though you're working, you didn't take his clothes to the dry cleaners, or you forgot to pick them up. Or, you got sirloin instead of rib eye, shopped at the wrong store, said the wrong thing, wore an ugly outfit, looked fat, and by the way, you're lousy in bed. And no matter how hard you try, it just never gets any better. In fact, it goes in the opposite direction and just gets a hell of a lot worse."

"But, I mean, you're such a smart woman and…"

"And so is your friend. Without meeting her, I'd guess you would describe her as smart, strong, personable, those sorts of things? And she's probably financially well off, right?

"Yeah, yes, to everything."

"Here's the deal. Austin Hackett is not unlike drug addiction. You know how they say the first high on cocaine is like an orgasm, only a thousand times more intense? Then you spend the rest of your addiction trying to reach that high again, but you never do, and very quickly, everything goes to hell. That's Austin. He sweeps you off your feet and then once that's done, he proceeds to convince you that you're just a piece of shit, and in the process, he takes all your money or at least tries to,"

"Was he violent?"

"He can be, but he makes you believe it's always your fault. Why did you make me hit you? Why did you make me lock you in the closet? Why did you make me tie you to the post in the basement?"

"He did that?"

"Yup, and you start to believe he's right. It was the same with all of us. I was his third wife. At least that we know of."

"You know Marcia Paxton and Constance Adams?"

"You have done your homework. Yeah, I know them. We have a survivors group. Their stories pretty much mirror mine except they took the abuse longer. I think Connie left him after four years, Marcia hung in there for almost two."

"I'd really like to talk to them. Could you give me their phone numbers? Maybe I could set something up and…"

"They both fled the state. I won't give you their phone numbers, but I'll pass yours on to them. Marcia's doing okay, I guess. Connie's pretty fragile."

"There must be something someone could do."

"Like I said, they fled the state, and I got a conceal and carry permit. That bastard comes anywhere near me, I'll shoot first, and he knows it. The best thing you can do is get to your friend. If you want some help, she and I can compare notes. He's probably got her on a short leash already, but she just doesn't realize it yet."

Thirteen

I didn't know either of the attorneys whose names were written on the bar napkin Louie had given me. After my uplifting meeting with Nancy Reilly, I called their offices the following morning. Pat O'Leary was in a conference, and Jack Griffith had a court appearance. I left a message for both. O'Leary called me back first.

"Haskell Investigations."

There was a slight pause before he responded. "This is Pat O'Leary. I'm returning a phone call from Devlin Haskell."

"You got him. Thanks for returning my call, Mr. O'Leary. May I call you Pat?"

"Depends on what this is about."

"It's regarding an attorney here in town, Austin Hackett."

"Hackett? Humph and you're working for him?" His tone had suddenly gone very hard.

"No, on the contrary. I'm looking into his details. I received your name as one of two individuals who battled him in court and won. The more I find out about him, the less impressed I'm becoming."

"Yeah, call me Pat. Hackett seems to have that effect on a lot of people. My case against him actually involved a shell company he operated called the Bunny Hutch. That's spelled as one word online."

I wrote that down as I spoke. "I've never heard that name before."

"Probably because it was a rather specialized practice, and it no longer exists."

"No longer exists?"

"Hackett filed for bankruptcy the day before the judgment against him came down."

"Would it be possible to meet?"

"To be honest, I'm really swamped. Is this is about Hackett?"

"Yes, but I think I can explain it a lot better in person. I'd be happy to meet you anywhere, anytime. It certainly doesn't have to be in your office."

"Tell you what, I'm in court all afternoon. If you can meet me at the courthouse, say twelve-thirty at the Kellogg Boulevard door, I can give you a few minutes."

"I'll see you there, twelve-thirty."

Fourteen

I was ten minutes early, standing just outside the re-volving door to the courthouse. A steady stream of people passed by on the wide sidewalk. It was a cloudless day, and the heat from the sun bounced off the Indiana limestone of the courthouse exterior, easily raising the temperature where I stood by another ten degrees.

A guy in a dark suit with grey hair pulled back in a ponytail took a half dozen steps out of the revolving door, then eyed me and said, "Haskell?"

Just as I asked, "Pat O'Leary?"

He extended his hand and gave me a firm shake.

"Nice to meet you. I appreciate you making the time," I said.

"Well, I haven't got much. Come on, we can talk on the way," he said then took off down the street. We walked a half-block toward a red wagon sitting at the curb advertising Chicago Hot Dogs. There was a line, maybe ten deep, waiting to order.

"You mentioned something called the Bunny Hutch," I said as we stepped to the back of the line.

"Actually, it was a shell organization Hackett had set up. I suppose you're looking into the disabilities suits. Bunny Hutch was his scam prior to that, or one of them. He supposedly made millions. He set up some off-shore companies, purchased the rights to a couple hundred porn movies, put the things out there hoping people would download them, and then sued when they did."

"He made money doing this?"

"Yeah, he brought a bunch of John Doe lawsuits under copyright infringement, then during the discovery process got access to the email accounts that downloaded the porn. That gave him access to individual emails, and then he just basically practiced extortion, threatening a lawsuit if they didn't settle."

"And that worked?" There were only about five folks ahead of us now, and the two guys in the wagon were dishing up hot dogs as fast as they could go.

"Almost always. Anyone who put up a fight usually had their case dropped. But thousands, we figure close to five hundred thousand, half a million folks, if you can believe it, settled for somewhere around two to four grand."

"You're kidding?"

"No, honest to God truth. Chances are the legal costs would run anyone at least as much, and even if they won the case, their name would be out there as having downloaded porn. The titles Hackett had the rights to, how should I say, were rather explicit. Nothing left to the imagination."

"And the few who did fight it?"

"Like I said, that's the ironic part. If the case actually went to court, Hackett would be losing money, so he'd just drop the lawsuit. But, if you were a minister, a school teacher, maybe an elected official or a public employee, would you want to take that chance and maybe lose your job for just a couple of grand? Do the math. Five hundred thousand people multiplied by two to four grand makes for a pretty nice income."

"Give me two, Tommy," O'Leary said, stepping to the window, then looked at me. "You gonna order anything?"

"I'll just have one," I said.

The guy took three buns and opened each in a separate cardboard tray. He placed a hot dog on the bun, then squirted a wiggly line of yellow mustard down the length of each dog, heaped on chopped white onions, tomato wedges, some peppers, pickle relish and added a pickle spear. It took him about thirty seconds to make the things. I paid for all three.

O'Leary said, "Thanks, Tommy." He headed for a knee-high wall running around the annex building and sat down. I followed.

"But he's not working that scam anymore?" I said and took a bite out of my Chicago Dog.

"No, the OLPR finally got wind of his scam, that's the Office of Lawyers Professional Responsibility. They went after him out in L.A., Ninth Circuit Court of Appeals. Anyway, the bastard declared bankruptcy to dodge court fines and the rest, as they say, is history."

He took another large bite finishing his first dog, licked his fingertips, then placed the empty cardboard tray beneath the second dog and started in.

"The more I find out about this guy, the more I'm amazed he's still out there walking around," I said.

"That may finally be coming to an end. I know the Minnesota Bar is looking at disbarment. He owes legal fees, penalties, payments to insurance companies, God only knows what else. I'd say look for him to try something big, and pretty soon. Word is he needs the cash."

I remembered Nancy Reilly's words, "He likes to strike while the iron's hot. There's probably a diamond ring in her not too distant future."

"You know anything about his personal life?"

O'Leary stared at me out of the corner of his eye for a brief moment. "Not first hand. He's been married more than once. Just a smaller version of his other scams. He seems to find a woman who believes him and has some income. He drains her bank accounts, and in the end, she just wants to get the hell away. Say, I had better get moving. Anything else I can help you with?"

"Yeah, how can you eat two of those things? I mean, they're good. In fact, they're great, but two?"

He smiled. "A little guerrilla combat. I'm in court in about fifteen minutes, nothing like breathing onion breath all over the guy on the opposite side," he said, then chuckled.

Fifteen

I was back in the office just a little after one. Louie was gone, and Morton was asleep. It didn't look like Morton had done any damage to the place while I was away. There were two messages waiting for me on the phone. One was from Jack Griffith, returning my call. The other was from AJ. Her curt message didn't sound all that promising. "Returning your call," she'd said, and hung up. I thought the better choice might be to call Griffith back.

I was on hold for a couple of minutes before he came on the line, "Griffith."

"Hello, Mr. Griffith, this is Dev Haskell. I'd left a message earlier, and you were kind enough to return my call. I apologize for not being in the office."

"You're a PI?" he asked

"Yes, I am," I said, hoping I'd disguised the surprise in my voice.

"Don't really have a need for that. I'll keep you in mind, but—"

"Hold on, Mr. Griffith. I just wondered if I could have a little of your time. I'm working on an investigation that seems to be growing by the minute, and your name came up."

"Is someone suing me?"

"No sir, actually it's in regard to a case you were involved in some time ago. I believe the defendant was a gentleman by the name of Austin Hackett."

"Hackett, for Christ's sake. First of all, that bastard's no gentleman."

"That would seem to be the common perception."

"What's he involved in now?"

"He's suing people under the Americans with Disabilities Act."

"He should be facing jail time for contempt, not to mention unethical behavior. I can only wish that was the reason for your call. What's he doing with the ADA?"

"I went on to explain what I knew, and how Hackett would threaten a six-figure lawsuit then offer to settle out of court for substantially less."

"Just another version of his unethical behavior. So, if I can cut to the chase here, instead of using the funds to get their business into compliance, Hackett is taking the settlement payment for himself, and neither improving the existing situation nor anything in the future, that about right?"

"That's what I suspect. I don't have any actual proof of that, but…"

"I normally wouldn't say this, but with Hackett involved, you don't need any proof. He's pulled this same routine before. It will take a while, but everything will eventually come crashing down on him. I'd say if there's any decency in the world, disbarment can't be too far down the road. Lord knows it's way overdue. I'm not sure, but I don't believe he can file for bankruptcy again, at least not yet. You're not working for him, are you?"

"No, thankfully."

"Cash upfront if you are," he chuckled.

"Actually, I'm working on a more personal aspect. An individual I know seems to be in a relationship with him. From what I've learned, he's capable of draining all her assets and leaving her with nothing."

"Oh, more than capable, but he'll leave her with something all right. Two things, as a matter of fact, a broken heart and one hell of a lot of debt."

"That's my fear."

"Nothing against your friend, but there always seems to be someone who falls for him, I could never quite figure that out."

Sixteen

We'd entered The Spot a few hours ago for just one. At this point, I'd lost count. "Another round, Jimmy," I said.

"It always amazes me that guys like this Hackett just keep on going. I tell ya, I forget to dot an 'i' or cross a 't,' and I'm hauled into chambers and filleted. That jerk just seems to keep on scamming," Louie said, then drained his glass just as Jimmy slid a fresh drink in front of him.

"Well, if it's any consolation, both the guys I talked to today gave the impression that he is on borrowed time."

"Borrowed time? That's been the case for at least a couple of years, but he's still out there scamming away."

"I'm going to check into that porn scam he cooked up. The one that was shut down out in LA."

"Yeah, 9th Circuit. No kidding. I think now they use the case as one of the examples in the law school ethics class. But, as I said, he's still out there, and apparently it hasn't slowed him down. What do you plan on telling Heidi?"

"That's my problem. I don't know what to tell her. Just about anything I say will sound like I'm making it up. I know her well enough to say she won't believe whatever I try to tell her unless I've got some really strong backup, and Woofy Barker isn't exactly the guy who's going to help me convince her."

"I'll be glad to help," Louie said, then drained half his drink.

"Yeah, thanks. It's just that she's so head over heels I'm afraid she'll just blow me off or think it's one last desperate effort to get her in the sack."

"Probably some truth to that last part."

"Well yeah, of course, but it's not the main reason."

"Always thinking of others," Louie smiled. "So, what's with the new girl, the one with the dog?"

"Well, she finally responded to my phone messages, in a way." I went on to tell him the tale.

"You see the common denominator here, no offense. I mean, we all like him, but Morton doesn't seem to be that conducive to your love life, at least where this woman is concerned."

"Yeah, she'll come around, I mean who ties a dog in heat up to a railing and then gets upset because another dog is riding her? What in the hell was she…" My cellphone suddenly gave off a wolf whistle tone. Louie and some guy a couple of stools down just stared at me. "Speak of the devil," I said, pulling the cell out of my pocket, "AJ. I think we'll just let her calm down a little more." I pushed the button that sent her into my message center.

"You think that was a good idea?" Louie asked.

The phone at The Spot rang a moment later, Jimmy answered on the third ring. "The Spot," he said then listened for a brief moment. "Let me see if he's here." There were six of us in the place, and three of us were at the bar.

"Some poor bastard's wife wondering where the hell he is," Louie said and drained his glass. I just shook my head in agreement.

Jimmy placed his hand over the receiver and said, "Dev, some woman on the phone, asking for you."

I almost spit my beer out, "What's she sound like?"

Jimmy gave a look, suggesting I was nuts. "She sounds like a woman, you know, a little higher pitched than you and me. You want the call or not?"

"Yeah, I better take it."

"Dumb shit," Louie said and pushed his empty glass toward Jimmy.

"It could be business. Hello?"

"Dev, it's AJ. I just tried to call you."

"You did? Oh, my phones over in the office. The battery was low, so I was recharging it for fifteen minutes before I went home."

Jimmy shook his head. Louie just stared off in the distance.

"Sure," AJ said, not sounding all that impressed. "Look, I wondered if you'd like to meet me tomorrow morning at the dog park. We could run the dogs, maybe have a moment to talk."

"Yeah, I'd like that, really like that."

"We'd just be talking, Dev and letting the dogs run."

"You just tell me where and we'll be there."

"It's on the bluff overlooking the river. You take Randolph down to Shepard Road then—"

"I know the place, I run Morton down there all the time," I lied. I'd been past the place a million times but never gone in.

"Would seven-thirty be too early? I've got a meeting at nine."

"Seven-thirty? No, not a problem, that works for me. We're up and usually on our walk by then."

"Okay, thanks, see you there."

"We'll be there, thanks for calling."

"Dinner, tomorrow night, way to go, man," Louie said and held his hand up to give me a high five.

"Actually, I'm meeting her tomorrow morning, in the dog park with Morton."

"The dog park? Another dating low. This is almost as bad as the time you took that woman to the morgue on the way to lunch. Didn't she just walk out and tell you never to call her again."

"Yeah, it didn't go too well. One of the BCA guys was there. Felt so bad, he gave her a ride home, then started dating her, and they ended up getting married. The best man mentioned me in his toast at the wedding

reception. I stood up and took a bow, got a lot of applause.”

"Incredible,” Jimmy said. “You want another?”

"No, I better get home. Early morning and I've got
to remember to set the alarm, so we get there on time.”

"See you tomorrow,” Louie said, then directed his
attention to the fresh drink Jimmy slid across the bar.

Seventeen

The alarm on the clock radio went off at six-thirty the following morning. Morton groaned then looked over at me. I climbed out of bed, walked over to the dresser, and turned off the alarm. "Come on, Morton, let's go, busy day."

He seemed to stretch with his eyes still closed then settled back down to sleep.

"Morton, come on, we got a date this morning, let's go,"

He looked at me like I was nuts, then gradually came off the bed once he realized I wasn't going to go away. He stood on all fours, stretched, and gave a long groan.

"Good boy, come on, let's go outside." I made sure he followed me down to the kitchen, where he stretched again while I held the door open for him. I turned on the coffee then hurried upstairs to shower. I pulled on a pair of reasonably clean jeans, got a not too wrinkled golf shirt out of the closet, filled a travel mug with coffee, and we were off. Morton managed to go back to sleep during the drive down to the dog park. We arrived ten minutes before AJ and Lady Godiva.

"Well, aren't you two the early birds. Been here long?" AJ asked, climbing out of her car. Lady Godiva was off her leash but walked perfectly alongside AJ. She ignored Morton bouncing back and forth next to her with a tennis ball in his mouth.

"Here, Morton, fetch the ball," I said, hoping he'd drop the ball, and I could toss it down the field. He didn't. In fact, he completely ignored me and focused his attention on Lady Godiva, obviously remembering their last meeting.

AJ gave a wave of her hand, and Lady Godiva sat, then laid down at her feet and remained oblivious to Morton, still jumping back and forth anxious for a play-mate. I half-grabbed him by the collar, then pried the tennis ball from his mouth. Now his quandary was, did he pay attention to the other dog or the guy with the tennis ball? I wound up like I was going to toss the ball, and he took off down the field. He turned after about twenty paces and barked as if to say, "Throw the thing, stupid."

"Can you release Lady Godiva to play?"

"Yeah," she said, and gave some command I didn't hear, and the dog was up and running out into the field. As she turned, I tossed the ball over their heads. Morton took off, but Lady Godiva was just that much faster. She grabbed the ball on the second bounce and took off down the field with Morton in hot pursuit.

"Wow, she's pretty fast. Hey, AJ, I'm really sorry about our last get together. I didn't mean..."

"Thanks, but it was really my fault. The signs were there;

I just wasn't paying attention. We went to the vet the next day and got everything taken care of just to be sure."

"Huh?"

"It's like a canine morning after pill."

"Oh, yeah, sure, of course."

Lady Godiva was now far down the field, leading Morton around in a circle.

"So, how have you been?" I asked.

"I recovered from the other day. In retrospect, it's kind of funny, although I wasn't seeing the humor of it at that particular moment."

I just nodded and figured it was best not to respond.

"You still working on that big investigation?"

"Yeah, although like most things in my business, it's boring background work. The guy I'm investigating seems to go from one scam to another, offers to settle out of court for about the same amount as folks would have to pay in legal fees. Kind of amazing some nut case hasn't gone after him."

"Or that the bar association hasn't censured him or something," she said, then glanced down the field, put two fingers in her mouth and gave a shrill whistle.

Both dogs seemed to stop in their tracks. Lady Godiva began to trot in our direction, and Morton dutifully followed.

"Actually, he was censured out in California on some previous scam. Rumor has it the Minnesota bar is looking into his latest activity, but as far as I know, they haven't actually done anything. Hey, I know you mentioned you've got a meeting this morning. You free for lunch?"

"Oh, Dev, that's so sweet. I'd love to, but there's a good chance my morning meeting may extend into the noon hour, and I have to keep my options open, sorry."

"Dinner?" I asked, half expecting her to be in church or helping the homeless or something.

"I can do dinner. How about just the two of us?" she said and smiled.

"I'd like that. You know where Desmond's is?"

"Yeah, that place with the paintings on the walls and the big fireplace? That would be perfect. I haven't been in there since, forever."

"That's it, see you there at seven-thirty. Just the two of us," I said and looked at Morton.

"Thanks for joining me this morning, Dev. I'm sorry if we seemed to have gotten off on the wrong foot the last couple of times. I…"

"Don't say another word. It's my fault, and thanks for giving me another chance. I missed your company."

"Oh, that's sweet," she said, leaned in, gave me a little kiss, then looked at Lady Godiva still holding the tennis ball and said, "Drop."

She dropped the ball immediately, whereupon Morton snatched it up and took off down the field. AJ laughed as she and Lady Godiva headed for their car. I spent the next ten minutes calling and whistling for Morton, who basically ignored me until he grew tired of running.

"So, how'd it go?" Louie asked. He was in shirt sleeves behind his picnic table desk, pounding away on his laptop.

"Better than I thought it would. I was half prepared to have her read me the riot act. She could not have been nicer, and in case you're interested, we have a dinner date tonight, just the two of us," I said, then watched Morton walk over to his bed and circle a couple of times before he flopped down for a nap.

"Well, there you go, and here I was thinking she was a smart woman. Actually, that's great. You find anything else out on your pal, Austin Hackett?"

"Nothing surprising. He seems to be universally disliked. Yet he still manages to always find someone, or a lot of someones, who buy into his scams."

"I may have found someone else you know who could be of help if you can find her," Louie said.

"Who's that?"

"Come here, tell me what you think," he said, then spun his laptop around so I could see the image on his screen.

Eighteen

It had been so long I'd forgotten what her real name was. The last time I'd seen her, she was dancing in one of Tubby Gustafson's strip joints, then holding hands with all the girls after closing time while she conducted a prayer session. She was a study in bad decisions and worse luck. She introduced herself on the website as Pepper and wanted you to just sit back and have a good time. Her voice sounded like she'd been screaming at a hockey game the night before. She occasionally seemed to slur her words, and it looked like she maybe staggered back and forth a bit. I first knew her by the name Swindle Lawless. After that, she'd been Cougar. And now here she was as Pepper, making it in the big time as the online spokeswoman for Austin Hackett's Bunny Hutch website.

"I thought the Bunny Hutch site was closed down. I Googled it, and I got this message on my screen that said the page was no longer available or couldn't be found, something like that."

"Guy I know gave me some software to kind of sneak in under the tent. The website is still out there, and always will be. It's just been blocked, at least for the average Joe."

"And you spotted Swindle?"

"Thought you'd find it interesting. I have to say it looks like her lifestyle is starting to take its toll."

The starburst pattern tattooed around Swindle's navel had been enlarged. Two fluttering hummingbirds had been added, one on either thigh with their long beaks extending into a flower tattooed on her lower region. A band of daisies was tattooed around one of her wrists. Her surgically enhanced chest was now pierced and, given the aging from forty-plus years of way too much sun on the rest of her body, appeared to be bolted on. She looked like she had four names tattooed on the side of her neck. All appeared to have a line running through them and were illegible, given the angle she was staggering from.

"What do you think?" Louie asked.

"I think it's amazing she's still alive. I'd like to find her and talk to her about Austin Hackett. Good Lord, first Woofy Barker and now Swindle Lawless. This guy Hackett must be looking under rocks to find these folks."

I phoned a guy I knew working on the vice squad and left a message. He called back about a half-hour later.

"Haskell Investigations."

"Hi Dev, Lester McKray. You called?"

In high school, we'd called him Lester the Molester, only because it rhymed. He was a straight shooter back then, and he still was today, although probably a lot more streetwise now than the majority of folks in town. I knew that during his off-hours, he gave counseling to runaway kids and had helped a number of them get off the street—One of the unsung heroes on the police force.

"Lester, thanks for returning my call. I'm looking for someone, she's come up in a case I'm working, I'm just trying to get background info. I'm not looking to arrest or haul her in or anything like that."

"Who is it?"

"Number of different stage names. She was dancing at one of Tubby Gustafson's joints under the stage name Cougar. I just saw her and—"

"You're kidding, Swindle Lawless? What do you want with her?"

I went on to explain my interest in Austin Hackett. I didn't mention Heidi's name.

"I've got her up on my computer now. God, just goes to show you what the lifestyle can do to you."

"At one point, she had a pretty major transformation, found Jesus or something. I thought she was going to turn over a new leaf."

"Yeah," Lester chuckled. "Then she convinced her minister that you have to sin before you can be saved. She basically shut down some born-again church single-handedly. Dozens of divorces, wife swapping parties, pretty much all due to Swindle."

"I'd love to talk to her and see what, if anything, she could tell me about Austin Hackett. Based on everyone else I've talked to, she'd have a story. There doesn't seem to be a lot of folks out there with something good to say about the guy."

"I know the name, but don't know anything about him, which I suppose is a good thing. You got a pen? I can give you her last known address. Her last run-in appears to be a booking for possession earlier this year. Looks like she did a couple of weeks in the workhouse. She's part of that ten percent of the population we seem to deal with on a weekly basis. Here you go…" Lester proceeded to give me the address, along with the apartment number. We chatted for another minute, then he wished me luck and got off the phone.

Nineteen

Swindle's apartment wasn't in the worst part of town, which actually came as a surprise. She was around the corner and up a half block from where the Tap Room bar used to stand. A cop had been shot inside the place about four years back, and the city tore down the entire structure, which did nothing but spread the slimy regulars to a half dozen other joints.

Swindle lived in a three-story red-brick building that was built over a hundred years ago. A large piece of red granite sat at the center of the roofline with the year "1912" carved in it. From the way the windows were positioned, I guessed the building was originally a six-unit structure. Based on the number of mailboxes set in the wall, there were eighteen much smaller units in there today.

A stack of discarded grocery circulars and direct-mail pieces had been tossed in a recycling box in the corner of the small entry. The box was overflowing, and the circulars now littered the better part of the floor. Yesterday had been the free recycling pickup on this end of town, but apparently, no one had been bothered enough to set the box out at the curb.

It was a little before one in the afternoon, and I pushed the buzzer next to the mailbox for unit thirteen. A scratchy female voice groaned out of the speaker, "You're early," then buzzed me through the security door without bothering to check who was there.

Her unit was up on the third floor and closest to the staircase. A couple of white garbage bags were leaning against the wall further down the hallway. From the smell, I guessed they'd been there for a while. By the look of the door frame on Swindle's unit, the door appeared to have been kicked in more than once. The upper tack on the '1' of '13' was missing, and the small brass number hung upside down. Someone had drawn a crude pornographic image on the wooden door with a black marker. A hole in the wall with two bare wires indicated where the doorbell used to be. I knocked.

The door opened a minute or two later, and there she was in the flesh, almost literally. She wore a black negligee that looked at least a size too large and hung down almost to her knees. The lace on the right side was torn, and a long strip dangled against her lower leg. She had a cigarette going in one hand and held a half-full glass of some clear liquid on ice in the other. I doubted it was water.

"You're awfully damn early. Come on in. We might as well get started," she said. From the tone of her voice and her posture, I guessed it wasn't her first meeting of the day.

"Hi, Swindle, how you been?"

"'Fraid you got it wrong, baby. I'm Pepper now, and I… Wait a damn minute, I know you, I think." She started to laugh, which immediately turned into a loud, hacking cough.

"Dev Haskell, Swindle."

"No, that's not it."

"Actually, yeah, it is. That's me."

"Really? Oh hell, you gotta be kidding me. Who knew? So, you come back for more, did ya? No wonder you're early, guess you just couldn't wait. Well, I tell you what, it's your lucky day 'cause I'm gonna give you a special, baby."

"Actually, I wanted to ask you some questions. I'm just looking for information on a guy, and…"

"Questions? You ain't a cop now, are you? I been good. You can just ask around. Everyone'll tell you I'm the best," she said, then started to laugh again, which brought her into another coughing fit.

I stepped inside, then closed the door behind me. A threadbare couch sat up against a grimy wall. What looked like an awfully new flatscreen that had to be sixty or sixty-five inches was no more than four feet from the couch. Beer cans, a couple of pizza boxes, and an almost empty plastic gin bottle littered the three-legged coffee table leaning against the far wall.

"Sure you ain't no cop?"

"No, Swindle, I'm not a cop. But your name came up as someone who might have some valuable information."

"That's me, Den, little Miss Valuable. Why don't you grab a seat and get comfortable while I just freshen up my drink? You want a little something?" she said, then raised her eyebrows, suggesting more than a beer.

"No, thanks, Swindle. I gotta watch myself."

"Oh, come on, we're old friends. Nothing you want that ain't been done before," she said and emptied the rest of the plastic gin bottle into her glass, filling it a good two-thirds of the way up. She took a couple of steps and opened the freezer compartment on her fridge, pulled out an ice cube tray, and set it on the counter. She tossed two cubes into her glass, causing it to overflow. She ignored the spill, left the ice cube tray on the counter, then sat down next to me. "Where do you want to start, Dave?"

"How about those names on your neck? That's a new addition since the last time we were together. What's that about?"

"Men, they're only after one thing," she said and took a healthy sip.

"So why put their name on your neck?"

"I want to look at it every day and never forget how they ripped me off. See?" she said then turned her head so I could read the names.

I'd been right. All four names were crossed out. The second one was Freddy, and I wondered if that was Fat Freddy Zimmerman, Tubby Gustafson's enforcer. The fourth name was Austin.

"That Austin, that's not Austin Hackett, is it? The guy with the Bunny Hutch website?"

"Let me tell you," she said, then made me wait while she took a big sip and stubbed her cigarette out in a pizza delivery box. "The bastard ripped me off. Promised me all sorts of business would come my way, and it never, ever did. Told me I was gonna be one rich bitch. Well, I got halfway there, and I ain't rich," she started to cackle then launched into another one of her coughing jags.

"He never paid you?"

"That wasn't exactly our deal. Well, see, he was going to send all sorts of movie producers my way, only he never did. Not so much as one little customer, not a one. Can you believe it?"

"So, what did you do?"

"I'm getting to that, honey, just give me a minute here," she said and fished a cigarette out of a crumpled pack at the end of the couch and stuck it between her thin lips. "Be a gentleman, won't you, Don?" she nodded toward a pack of matches resting next to the pizza boxes.

I opened it up, noticed a phone number written on the inside, then lit her cigarette, and stuffed the pack into my pocket. Swindle, ever the lady, blew a cloud of smoke up toward the burnt-out bulb hanging from the dingy ceiling.

"Bastard promised me it was going to be the chance to restart my career in Hollywood. Get noticed by the big names, you know, movies, maybe an Academy Award or something."

"You were out there once before, weren't you?"

"Hollywood? Yeah, I made a bit of a name for my-self," she said, then sat up a little straighter and pushed a greasy lock of hair off her forehead. Girl Overboard, Teacher's Pet, Spanky, Stroke Machine, ever see 'em?"

"Afraid not."

"You should check 'em out, they're hot. I starred in all of 'em plus a bunch I can't seem to recall just now," she said, furrowing her brow in an effort to remember. "Oh well, it don't really matter. Anyway, that rat Austin promised me a contract and introduction to some big names. I never heard a damn thing. So, I decide I'm gonna get in touch with him, let him know he ain't just screwing some virgin."

"I'm sure he didn't think that, Swindle," I said be-fore I could stop myself.

She didn't blink. "So I went to his office, then I went to his home. Told some bimbo who said she was his housekeeper that I wasn't leaving until I got a starring role. Next thing I know, some bad boy ties me up, tosses me in the trunk of a shiny black limo, and keeps me in a cabin for a week with him and his pals."

"Keeps you in a cabin?"

"Yeah, up in the woods somewhere, big fancy place. We started to party, and I wore every one of 'em out. Then once the fools figured out I was a lousy cook, they brought me back to town, gave me a couple hundred bucks, and promised to stop by every-now-and-again."

"And do they stop by?"

"Like I said, every-now-and-again."

"Did you know Austin Hackett was a lawyer?"

"A lawyer? You gotta be kidding me. When'd he start that? He's a film producer, least that's what he told me, had a bunch of them triple-X movies set up for his website. That's why he hired me, cause I got a name. I'm famous, kind of, in certain circles."

"You ever think of going to the police?"

"You think I'm crazy? Bastards'll just arrest me like they always do. Fancy shits like Austin, them rich pricks, they always get away with whatever they do. Go to the cops, what the hell are you smoking?" she said, then drained a good portion of her drink. The buzzer suddenly rang on her intercom.

"Now who in the hell would that be? You're here early and now my three o'clock, hell it ain't even two. That's just crazy. Hey, what do ya say to a three-way?"

"No, thanks, Swindle. Tell you what. I appreciate your time. I'll let you get on with the business at hand." I pulled a couple of twenty-dollar bills out of my pocket and tossed them on the coffee table.

"Mmm-mmm, thanks, honey. Listen, you ever want to come back and chat, you just let me know. Always willing to work something out for a generous kind of man," she said, then placed a hand on my shoulder and started to tickle my ear.

I quickly grabbed her hand and shook it. "Thanks for the time, Swindle."

"Remember, it's Pepper, now honey. Listen, if I can help you getting Austin, you just let me know. I'll make it worth your while," she said, then winked as she picked up the twenties and stuffed them beneath the cushion on the couch. The buzzer on the intercom rang again, this time much longer.

"I better head out and let you get back to work. Many thanks," I said and quickly hurried out the door. I could hear her groaning into the intercom as the door closed behind me.

"You're early, baby…"

I passed a middle-aged fat guy on the second floor. He was red-faced and breathing heavy, resting for a minute before he climbed up the final flight of stairs. I could only hope he knew what he was getting into.

Twenty

I sat behind the wheel of my car and pulled out the pack of matches from Swindle's apartment. For all I knew, the phone number could be a pizza delivery guy, but I dialed it anyway.

After a couple of rings, a husky voice answered, "This is Clarence."

"Hi Clarence, my name is Dev Haskell. I got your number from a woman named Pepper."

"The movie star?"

I had to think a moment. "Yeah, I guess that's her. I was wondering if we could talk."

"Talk?"

"I'm doing some investigation for a lawsuit. I'm not an attorney. I'm not a cop. I—"

"So, you're like a private investigator or something?"

"Actually, yeah. That's it exactly. I'm investigating an individual by the name of Austin Hackett."

"Oh yeah, sometime client of mine. A lot of people seem to be unhappy with him."

"That would appear to be the general opinion. Would it be possible to meet you somewhere?"

"Tell you what. I'm working right now. In fact, I better get off the line here, but I've probably got some downtime early this evening."

"You name the place, and I'll be there."

"There's a Subway shop corner of Selby and Victoria. I should be there right around six."

"I'll be there. How will I know you?"

"You can't miss me," he said and hung up.

I brought Morton home a little before five, took him for a nice long walk, got his dinner ready, then headed toward the Subway shop. It wasn't too far from my place.

About ten minutes after I arrived, a black limo pulled into the parking lot. The limo driver was a large man with skin the color of creamy coffee. He was dressed in a dark suit with epaulets on the shoulders. He wore a black hat with a patent leather visor. As he walked in the door, someone from behind the counter called, "Evening, Clarence."

I walked up behind him and said, "I'll get this, and I'll have the same, too."

"That okay with you, Clarence?" the guy behind the counter asked, then eyed me.

Clarence nodded and held out his hand, "You must be the gentleman that called me earlier, Clarence Rutherford."

"Dev Haskell, Clarence. Nice to meet you."

We walked back to a corner table. Clarence gave the nod to a couple of different folks in the place. We sat down, and he proceeded to unwrap his sandwich. "Listen, Dev, I got a busy night, concert downtown, and I'm moving five different groups, so unfortunately, I can only give you a few minutes."

"Not a problem, I understand. How do you manage to shuffle five groups in your limo?"

"I own five limos," he smiled then took a large bite of his sandwich.

"Austin Hackett. So what can you tell me?"

"Humph, well, my dealings with him have probably been better than most. That's only because I have him on a cash upfront basis. You're in this business for any amount of time you get to size folks up rather quickly. Austin Hackett is cash upfront."

"You chauffeur him around a lot?"

"Almost never. I don't really know the particulars, but my guess is he uses my service as window dressing just trying to impress folks. It's part of the business, a lot of folks do that. I do a lot of pickups at the airport, dropping folks off at someone's office then bringing them back for a flight out of town. Almost always the same day. That's invariably the kind of work I do for Mr. Hackett."

"What about Pepper?"

"Pepper, she was a little different story. One of my employees brought her up to Austin's lake place for a couple of days, along with three or four other individuals. Not sure of the circumstances exactly. If I remember correctly, after four or five days, he drove back up there, took the *gentlemen* to the airport, and Miss Pepper to her home."

"You know anything about Hackett's business?"

"Oh, you hear things. You know, you drive folks around. After a bit, they just act like you aren't there, and then they start talking."

"What'd you pick up?"

"Nothing I'd really care to share. What's the term, client confidentiality, and all? I hear enough to know Mr. Hackett will remain a cash upfront customer, and as long as that's the case, I'll be happy to provide him with our service."

"Fair enough. You aware of any security on his part?"

"Security?" Clarence said then seemed to suddenly grow a little wary.

"At his office, his home? Does he have people, a bodyguard anything like that?"

"Nothing beyond the normal things. He's got an alarm system at his home, and a fence with a big gate surrounding the property. His office building has a desk with a couple of security guards down in the lobby, but you just check with them, and then they call up to announce you. There's something like twenty floors with different offices in the building, so it's nothing unusual. I've never picked up on anything like a bodyguard. What's he done, anyway?"

I gave Clarence the cliff note description. I didn't mention Heidi or anyone else for that matter.

"Not surprising. There's a certain bunch of folks, clients of mine, you know they're involved in certain things, but that's just the business. That bothers you, well then you shouldn't be driving a limo. It's like lawyers. They deal with criminals, but they're highly regarded, and I suppose that's fair, I guess. Long as they pay their bill and they aren't doing anything illegal in my vehicles, I don't have a problem."

We said goodbye out in the parking lot. I grabbed a couple of Clarence's cards, not that I planned to use a limo anytime soon, but you never know. I tossed the half of a Subway I couldn't eat into the front seat of my car and headed home.

Something was bothering me as I sat on the couch, sipping a beer in my den, but I couldn't get a handle on exactly what it was. I'd gone over my conversation with Clarence a half dozen times, but wasn't coming up with anything. The Twins were playing Chicago, actually doing pretty well, although it was only the bottom of the second inning when my phone gave off the wolf whistle. AJ calling.

"Hello."

"Did you forget our date?" There wasn't a polite tone to her question.

Twenty-one

I started pouring and said, "Like I just told you, I was involved in this stakeout at a suspected bank robber's house, at least we think he's a dangerous bank robber. Anyway, I'm hiding in his closet and had the phone turned off, so I couldn't text you. He was supposed to leave at six, something got screwed up. I'd just gotten cleaned up at home and was ready to phone you when you called. More wine?"

"Careful, you don't have to fill it to the rim. Just let me sip this. So if you were home getting cleaned up, how come you're in the same jeans and that, that shirt with the food stain you had on this morning?"

"Oh, well, see, I didn't want to waste time putting a different outfit on, and, well, I was rushing around so I could get over here."

"Why didn't you just call?"

"Yeah, I should have done that. I guess I was just thinking of being with you, and so my mind blocked out all other options."

She just let that last line hang out there, sat back, sipped her wine, and studied me, slowly nodding her head.

"What?"

"I'm thinking you're a lot of work."

"Too much work?"

"I'm not sure."

"Would you care to order an appetizer?" The waitress asked, saving me from further grilling at least for the moment.

"None for me," AJ said, more or less setting the tone.

"I think I'll have the Thai chicken with the peanut sauce."

"Oh, you better not get that…"

"Relax, AJ. You don't have to have any if you don't want to. On the other hand, if you want to try some, you can help yourself. Fair enough?"

"No, not really. See I…"

"Hey, AJ, I'm sorry I was working…"

"In a closet."

"Well, yeah, but in my business, sometimes it's gets kind of weird. I'm sorry I was late. I'd like to make it up to you somehow. It's just that I don't want to see you unhappy for the rest of the night. If you'd feel better just going home and not being here for dinner, I wouldn't like it, but you can just head home and not have to put up with me. Especially, if I'm upsetting you. No pressure, I'm not yelling, I just don't want to upset you."

"You're not upsetting me, Dev. It's just, oh, I don't know, it just seems like there's some ulterior force that keeps screwing things up between us. It's almost like it's written in the stars that we aren't supposed to be together or something."

"Really? Written in the stars? You're kidding me?" I laughed.

Fortunately, AJ laughed, too. "Well, you have to admit, it's been more than a little crazy."

"Well yeah, but so far, it's all been my fault."

"You just keep thinking like that, it's always your fault, and there might still be a chance for us," she said, then raised her glass and we toasted the fact that it would always be my fault.

"Your appetizer, sir." the waitress said and set a small plate in front of me with three skewers of chicken bits and the peanut sauce that I love.

"You sure you won't try one?" I asked AJ.

"No, no thanks," her voice seemed to raise an octave, and she pushed back in her chair, getting as far away as possible from the plate. I figured she must have had an incident with a chicken as a kid.

"Are you ready to order?"

AJ seemed to relax and ordered something in French I couldn't pronounce. I ordered a steak, rare.

We seemed to reach a happy medium once the food arrived. She stopped giving me the third degree on why I'd been late, which allowed me to stop making up stories and then try to remember what I'd told her ten minutes earlier. She took little bites of her creme brûlée dessert after tapping the melted sugar top with her spoon. I graciously shared my ice cream with the caramel sauce.

The night seemed to have finally landed on the right foot, and she was smiling and laughing when applause erupted from the far side of the dining room.

Someone shouted, "Bravo," and a couple of women seem to sigh. I had to turn around in my chair to look across the room, and although the guy with the spiked hair looked familiar, I was having trouble placing him. The woman sat with her back to me, dark hair with crazy blonde highlights. She turned around, smiled, and said something to the table behind her. She placed a hand on her upper chest and gave half a shrug. Heidi.

"Dev. Dev, hello."

"What? Oh, sorry, it's just that I think I know that couple and—"

"The one that just got that necklace. I was watching. He just gave her the thing. It must have been a surprise. Oh, that's so romantic."

"He gave her a necklace?"

"Yeah," AJ said, scraping the last bit of creme brûlée out of the little dish. "That's why everyone was clapping. God, I bet it's diamonds, lucky lady. You know them?"

"Yeah, I should probably go over and say congratulations. Do you want another dessert?"

"No, you go on. I'll just wait, but don't stay too long."

I headed over to their table, as the surrounding area returned to normal. Heidi's back was facing me, so she didn't see me approach. Austin Hackett gave me a dismissive glance, then paid a lot more attention once I stepped around the table next to them and stopped.

"Just wanted to say that was pretty classy, congratulations," I smiled and held out my hand.

"Thanks, but I'm the lucky one."

Heidi looked up at the sound of my voice. "Dev?" she said and put her hand up to what looked like a dazzling diamond necklace.

"Heidi, oh my God. So you're the lucky lady. Well then, you must be Austin Hackett. I've heard a lot about you."

"Hopefully, all good," Hackett said and forced a laugh.

"Dev, what the hell are you doing here?"

"The same thing as you, having dinner. My date is just over there." All three of us turned just as AJ set her wine glass down and gave a little wave.

"Oh, my, very pretty," Heidi said. I knew her well enough to realize she meant anything but, the tone of her voice had morphed from happy to a razor-sharp edge in a matter of one short sentence.

"And you are?" Hackett said, breaking off the stare between Heidi and myself.

"Oh, sorry. Haskell, Dev Haskell. Heidi and I have known one another for a long time. Hey, I'll let you two get back to your evening. Congratulations, really nice gift. You'd better get that appraised and insured Heidi. You never know nowadays."

"Already taken care of," Hackett said. "Nice meeting you, Hanson."

"Enjoy the night," I said, then hurried back to AJ.

"Wow, what did you say? He's looking over here and doesn't appear too happy."

"Oh, that guy, he's just some shyster lawyer I ran into a while back. Rumor has it he may be doing some time in the near future."

"Really?" AJ said and stared across the room at Hackett.

"You ready to head out?"

"What? Well, yeah, I suppose, I mean if you want to. Would you like to maybe come over to my place for a nightcap or something?" she asked.

"Yes, I'd like that a lot." I paid the bill, gave a final glance at Heidi and Hackett. I made a silent vow I'd help put him away for a long time, then headed out the door with AJ. I walked her to her car, held the door for her, and then forcibly pulled her to me and gave her a big hard kiss. She seemed to struggle for a brief moment, then wrapped her arms around me and kissed back, just like in the movies.

"Oh, wow, let me catch my breath. Hurry over if you've got more of that," she said.

I closed the door, waved at her as she drove off, walked to my car, and followed just a minute or two behind her. I figured I would catch up to her, but I never did. I ended up waiting in front of her place. After three unanswered phone calls over the course of forty-five minutes, I drove home.

Twenty-two

My cellphone gave off the wolf whistle announcing AJ on the line just a little before six the following morning. I flew out of bed, not that I'd slept much during the previous night between worrying back and forth about AJ and Heidi. Morton stretched out just enough to take up virtually all the room on the bed and gave me a look that suggested, "Answer that damn thing."

"AJ, you okay?"

"I am now. Actually, I'm in the hospital."

"The hospital? What happened? Did you have an accident? I didn't see anything on the road, and I was literally just a minute or two behind you. Is the car okay? How are you? I—"

"Dev, Dev, it's all right. Calm down. I just had an allergic reaction is all."

"Allergic reaction? To what, the wine?"

"No, it…"

"Don't tell me it was the creme brûlée."

"No, it was you."

"Me?"

"Yeah, kind of funny. You're just the carrier, so to speak. I have a peanut allergy, a severe peanut allergy."

"Peanuts?"

"Yes, I swell up, I mean right now I look like I went three rounds with Mike Tyson. My lips are huge. My eyes are almost swollen shut, my skin is all blotchy, but I'm in the recovery mode at this point. I felt it coming on about thirty seconds after you kissed me. I stopped to turn at the corner and just thought oh-oh. When you had that peanut sauce on your appetizer, I knew it was going to be trouble, but I just hoped, well, you know, as long as I didn't actually eat any of it, I was hoping I'd be okay. Now everyone can see how well that worked."

"Are you in any pain?"

"No, they gave me an epinephrine injection and kept me overnight for observation. I didn't think I'd make it home in time to get to my meds. Now they're just waiting for the swelling to go down, and then I can get out of here. Hopefully, they'll release me this afternoon."

"All because I kissed you?"

"Relax, I should have known better."

That didn't sound good. "What hospital are you in."

"I don't want you coming down here."

"Regions?"

"No."

"United?"

"No."

"Oh, so it's St. Joseph's."

"I don't want you seeing me like this. I'm an absolute mess."

"And I'm the one who apparently did it to you."

"Not to worry. I just didn't want you thinking I stood you up or something because of that other woman."

"Other woman? You mean, Heidi? I just have known her for a long time. The guy she's with is a real creep, and he's liable to try and drain her bank accounts."

"Drain her bank accounts? And you know this how, exactly? I mean, he gave her diamonds last night, didn't he?"

"They're most likely fake, and I know all this because I've spoken to a former wife of his, a couple of people he cheated in business and two attorneys who fought the jerk in the courtroom."

"But, it was so romantic, you know at the restaurant. I mean, you heard everyone clapping."

"It was all staged, AJ. Part of his deal is he has false insurance papers, so she won't get the diamonds appraised because they're always fake, just cubic zirconium and worth about twenty bucks."

"You're kidding. It sounds like you're stalking or something. I— Oh, hey, my doctor is just coming in. I gotta run. Bye, bye, bye," she said then hung up the phone.

I made breakfast, let Morton out, showered, shaved, and headed down to St. Joseph's hospital. AJ was still there, up on the third floor, and not all that happy to see me.

"I told you not to come," she said then pulled the bed sheet up over her head.

"To tell you the truth, I expected worse. You don't look that bad."

"Really?" she said, lowering the sheet to about her nose and peeking out with puffy eyes.

"Yeah, no kidding. It looks like the swelling is way down," I lied.

"Way down?"

I forged ahead. "So, you're getting out this afternoon?"

"Yeah, unless something changes, but it seems to be getting back to normal. They've got me scheduled for an afternoon release once they check me after the noon hour."

"You ought to take a picture now, then maybe another tomorrow at the same time, post it online and tell everyone you've been working out and lost a lot of weight."

"Do you think I look fat?"

"No, just the swelling, it—"

"Great, so I do look fat. God, I should probably wear a ski mask out of here, so no one recognizes me."

"Yeah, a ski mask, I'm sure that wouldn't attract anyone's attention. What about Lady Godiva? Is anyone taking care of her?"

"Wow, amazing. Maybe you do have a sweet gene. Thanks for asking, but my sister's on it. She's probably over there right now."

"Okay, but if she's not or can't make it or whatever, you just give me a call, and I'll run over."

"Sure, I appreciate that. Really, I do. Listen, thanks for coming down, and thanks for dinner last night, Dev. I mean it, but I'd kind of like to just quietly recover if it's all the same."

"Yeah, dinner worked out really well," I said and indicated the hospital room we were in.

"Well, no offense, but I might just take a pass on a kiss until another day. I'll give you this much. Life is certainly an adventure with you, Dev. A real adventure."

"Yeah, stick with me. Who knows? Once in a while, it might even turn out to be a little fun."

"I'm going to hold you to that, mister."

"You ain't seen nothing yet."

"That's what scares me, Dev."

Twenty-three

As soon as I left the hospital, I drove home to pick up Morton then headed down to the office."

"Banker's hours for the two of you?" Louie said.

"God, you won't believe it," I said then proceeded to fill him in over a cup of really bad coffee.

"Could it get any worse?" he laughed.

"It did," I said, and told him the part about Heidi.

"Well, now he knows you're out there. He might just let it go, but my sense is he'll try and mix things up for you, create some pain in the ass problem just to keep you occupied. Then before you know it, he's whisked her off somewhere, they get married, and she wakes up in the not too distant future and finds herself without a penny to her name."

"That sounds like what Jack Griffith said about Hackett. He leaves all the women with two things, a broken heart and a hell of a lot of debt."

"Unfortunately, I don't think that's an exaggeration," Louie said.

My cellphone rang; the incoming number came across as unknown.

"Haskell Investigations."

"Dev?"

"Heidi, is that you?"

"Yes, I just wanted to chat with you for a moment. It was nice to see you last night. I'm sorry you couldn't join us, but Austin gets so jealous whenever another man pays the least bit of attention to me. He really needs to know there's no one else but him."

"So, stopping by to congratulate the two of you, even when I'm with another woman, that's too much attention?"

"You don't have to be like that, Dev. That's not what I meant."

"What did you mean, Heidi?"

"Dev, I just wanted to call and thank you for saying congratulations. To tell you the truth, when I saw you, I didn't know how you'd handle it, didn't know what to expect from you. You've always been, well, you were always there for me picking up the pieces following one failed love affair after another. And I maybe never told you, but I always appreciated that."

"It's always been my pleasure, Heidi. You've always been important. I just don't want to see you hurt. That's my only concern."

"Hurt? Dev, I finally have someone in my life who doesn't look at me like I'm just the next roll in the hay."

"I never looked at you like that."

"Oh, really? Who are you trying to kid? Besides, it was mutual, and I loved every minute of it, except for that New Year's you had too much to drink and threw up. Then there was the time…"

"I get it, Heidi. You didn't have to bring that New Year's Eve up," I said, but at least she was laughing.

"Well, just thanks for being there all those times and even last night. It was really sweet of you."

Imagine that, me being called sweet twice in the same day. "I'm happy for you if you're happy. It's just that things seem to be moving awfully fast. I don't know, Heidi, maybe you could slow things down a little."

"Slow things down, and that's coming from you. How many times did we climb in the backseat of the car in some dark parking lot because you just couldn't wait or—"

"I don't know that we need to be going into that specific detail. What I meant was, well, just you know, check things out."

"Check things out?"

"Yeah, like maybe does he have any previous marriages? What's the status of his law practice? Some due diligence, you know, like you'd do if he was one of your prospective clients. You wouldn't do business with a potential investor without a financial report."

"An investor? Like I'm something that can just be bought and sold? Is that what you're suggesting?"

"No, no, nothing like that. It would just seem to me that you would want to make sure he's, you know, on the level. Check it out. I mean, was he really a Navy Seal?

Did he nurse his parents until they passed away? Was he ever married? What can it hurt?"

"Trust, Dev. In the end, that's what it's all about. Not everyone is like the people you deal with. Not everyone is looking for the fast buck, the short cut, the easy way. I'll have you know, Austin works extremely hard to ensure that handicapped individuals, that's right, people not as fortunate as you or me, he works awfully damn hard to make sure they get a fair shake. And when he finds someone who's screwing them, he gets aggressive, Dev. Because he doesn't like to see the little guys, the folks without the resources get pushed around. So he stands up for them and makes people comply with the law. It's the goddamn law, Dev." She was shouting now.

"Do me a favor, Heidi. You know those diamonds you got last night. The gift from your fine upstanding lover, take them somewhere and get them appraised. See what they're worth. Then call me back."

"Oh," she screamed and hung up.

"That didn't sound like it went all that well," Louie said.

"This jerk's got her really buffaloed."

"I could hear her yelling all the way over here."

"I just wish she'd go and get those damn diamonds appraised. She'll find out they're fakes and we can start to get her thinking again. It's like she won't even listen to reason."

"Can I make a suggestion?"

"I don't want to kidnap her."

"That wasn't what I was going to suggest. However, if you nicely suggested getting together and then calmly talked to her, without making accusations, maybe things might turn out a little better."

"You heard her screaming, defending that piece of shit. How am I supposed to deal with that?"

"I think you're going to have to find a way if you want to get through to her. You're the one who said time is running out. What did that ex-wife say? He strikes when the iron's hot? I'd say it's steaming right about now, pal. You're going to have to suck it up and just do it."

"Okay, okay, I'll do it," I said, although I had what seemed like a lot better idea just beginning to percolate.

Twenty-four

little after six the following morning, I was parked down the street from Heidi's house. Morton was in the backseat happily gnawing away on the rawhide chew toy I'd given him. Heidi hurried out her front door around nine, looking like a million bucks, jumped in her little red BMW and took off down the street. I decided to wait for a bit on the odd chance she'd forgotten something and decided to return.

After ten minutes, we got out of the car and walked up the block to her place. I had Morton on a leash, pretending to be a local just out walking his dog. He carried the rawhide in his mouth, not about to let go. More than once after I'd spent the night, she'd kissed me good-bye and told me to let myself out as she dashed off to work. So on the odd chance that scum bucket Austin was lingering inside, I rang the doorbell.

Morton tugged at his leash, but I was focused on the far side of Heidi's front door, straining my ears to hear any movement. I rang the doorbell a couple more times. Morton continued to tug on the leash and barked, and I continued to ignore him. She'd given me a spare key to her house some years back when she'd spent the better part of a winter down in Florida. I'd found the key in a desk drawer last night around two in the morning after searching through my entire house. I stepped back, tied Morton's leash to the railing on the front steps, then unlocked the door.

"Heidi," I called as I stepped into her entryway. "Heidi, it's Dev." No one answered. Heidi's entryway had a marble floor, some special Italian marble she just loved. Creamy-colored wall to wall carpeting that was wonderfully plush and "cost a small fortune" covered the living room floor and continued down the hallway to her bedroom. I carefully walked through the living room, ears perked for the slightest noise. I stopped at her bedroom door and slowly peeked around the corner, just in case that dipshit Austin was in bed. He wasn't. The room was empty. I hurried over to her triple chest of drawers, opened the top middle drawer, and pulled out the box she kept her special jewelry in. The box was some family heirloom, antique, and made of dark walnut with a lid that was inlaid with mother of pearl. Heidi once told me it had been in her family for something like five generations.

I'd always suggested to her that maybe she should hide the damn thing so some low-life wouldn't come in and take it. But what would I know? She never seemed to listen, and so now that was exactly what was happening.

I set the box on top of the chest of drawers and slowly opened the lid. There it was, close to two dozen stones in the shape of an inverted triangle. The stones grew larger in each row with a nicely sized stone at the bottom and an even larger stone dangling from that. They may have been fakes, but even I had to admit, it was beautiful. The fake setting looked like silver.

I placed the necklace in my pocket, returned the box to the drawer, then turned to hurry out of the room. That's when I saw my footprints or rather, a footprint. Not the whole foot, thank God, but enough of a trail. I quickly slipped my shoes off and looked at the sole of the right foot. Thanks, Morton. I'd tracked just enough from the front door across the living room, down the hallway, and into the bedroom leaving a direct trail. Shit. Literally.

I didn't have time to worry about it just now. I carried my shoes out to the front stoop where Morton had left his signature pile. I remembered him pulling at his leash and the bark. I must have been so focused on the front door, hoping Austin Hackett wouldn't appear that I wasn't paying attention. I'd just have to deal with it later and hurried off to the jewelers.

* * *

"Nice, very nice," the jeweler said, then set the glass he was looking through on the counter and smiled. He wore a grey suit, a starched white shirt, and a navy blue tie. The lights from the ceiling fixture glistened off his bald head, giving the sense of a halo. "I can have a value estimate for you in forty-eight hours."

"Forty-eight hours? I was hoping for maybe like noon today. See, we've got to catch a flight for a funeral, and she wanted to wear this."

"Oh, sorry, my condolences. Noon? Gee, we couldn't do that, but, well, if we put a rush on it, I could probably have that for you, oh, say by three. What time's your flight?"

"Five, that's cutting it short, but yeah, let's do that. I just want to call the insurance folks, get it covered before we travel, you know." Besides, once you realize it was a fake.

"Now, there'd be a modest rush fee, just fifty dollars, and I can give you a credit toward your next purchase."

Heidi was worth fifty bucks. "That's fine. I'll see you at three."

* * *

I hosed off her front stoop then hurried inside to attack the damage I'd done to her carpet. I started in the bedroom, which seemed to go more or less okay. By the time I reached the hall, the offending material had been removed, but there was a larger stain beginning to appear where I'd scrubbed. It all seemed to look worse the closer I got to the front door. There was no 'more or less' about it, by the time I'd worked my way into the living room. I went over my trail three different times. Each time, working with a bucket and a sponge, I just seemed to make the stain a little larger. I'd have to shampoo the carpet, which meant it wouldn't be dry before she came home. God, what the hell else could go wrong?

* * *

"I have to tell you, Mr. Haskell, this piece is quite exquisite."

That wasn't exactly what I'd expected to hear. He had the necklace sitting on top of a piece of black velvet next to a very formal looking appraisal sheet.

"You estimated the value at twenty-four thousand dollars?" I looked up into his smiling face and the halo shining off his head.

"Yes, and to be honest," he lowered his voice to almost a whisper. "That's a tad on the conservative side."

"I don't believe it. They're real? I was thinking cubic zirconium. You gotta be kidding me. You're sure about this? You double-checked?"

He couldn't hide the stunned look on his face. "Cubic? Oh no, you've three carats in those bottom two stones alone. Very high quality, the cut, the color, certainly one of the better pieces we've seen over the past few years. If you were thinking of selling, I can tell you we'd be very interested. Of course, we couldn't match the estimated value, but still, it might be worth your while." He nodded in a way that seemed to suggest my

St. Paul Saints t-shirt and the jeans with the wet knees might be interested in an offer.

"You're sure about this?"

"Quite, sir."

I shook my head, stuffed the necklace into my pocket, and stood there stunned.

"Now there is the matter of the rushed appraisal, sir. That will be fifty dollars," he said, then followed up with a quick smile.

"Oh, yeah, sorry, it's just that, God, I can't believe it."

"Always a bit of intrigue in this business, sir."

Twenty-five

I needed to buy some time. I'd returned the piece to Heidi's jewelry box, shampooed her carpet, and set up a couple of fans turned on as fast as they'd go to hopefully speed up the drying process. Just now, I was sitting on her front stoop with the sun beating down on me. I was sweating, but it had nothing to do with the temperature when I phoned her.

"Dev?" she answered.

"Hi, Heidi, do you have a moment to chat?"

"I suppose," she said, then waited for me to talk. I envisioned her crossing her arms with a look on her face that suggested go ahead, idiot.

"Look, I'm sorry about our earlier conversation, I..."

"Conversation? Is that what it was, a conversation?"

"No, that's not what it was. It was me getting upset because I feel like I'm losing you. I know I drive you crazy, but, well, I guess I'd always hoped it would be me. As happy as I am for you, and I'm happy," I lied, "at the same time, I'm sad. You have to admit, we've had a lot of fun together."

"I don't believe it."

"Huh?"

"You actually have a heart, you creep. Thank you."

"Look, could we just meet and chat, maybe an early dinner tonight?"

"Early dinner?"

"Yeah, how about near your office, before you head home? Just the two of us. Afterward, you can take off, and I won't goof up whatever plans you have for the rest of the night."

"I should probably check with Austin, first."

This was not the Heidi I knew. "If you think you should. I mean, you could be home by seven at the latest." I was praying her carpet would be dry by then.

"Tell you what, you know Mario's?"

"That little restaurant in your building?"

"Yes, just meet me there at five. I'll phone Austin and let him know."

"I was hoping it would just be the two of us."

"It will be. I just need to touch base is all. I'll see you then," she said and hung up.

So far, so good. I took my shoes off on the front stoop, then went back in her house, and double-checked the flowers I'd set out on her kitchen table. I positioned the congratulatory card I'd written against the vase, and then hauled the rug cleaning equipment I'd rented out to my car. If she questioned me, I'd tell her I just thought it would be a nice thing to do.

By the time I returned the rental equipment, I barely had thirty minutes before I had to meet Heidi. I hurried home, grabbed a shower, threw on some pants and a clean shirt, and hurried down to Mario's. The bartender was just sliding my beer across the bar when Heidi walked in.

"Hey, what can I get you?"

She just stared at me.

"What?"

"Your shirt, it's inside out."

"It is?" I said, then looked down. The embroidered patch on the left breast was just a white tag with the letters running backward. "Oh, sorry about that," I said, then pulled the shirt off and turned it right side out and slipped it back on. "There."

"Incredible. Do you know what would happen if I did that?"

"You mean take your shirt off? Yeah, every guy in the building would line up to buy you a drink."

"You're still the same," she said and gave me a kiss on the cheek.

We chatted for the better part of an hour, largely just reminiscing about things we'd done, places we'd been, people we'd known. She seemed happy enough, although we hadn't really broached the subject of Austin Hackett yet. The chat was beginning to feel more and more like a funeral to me, and after the disappointing news on the jewelry appraisal, I wasn't sure bringing up Austin was the best idea.

"Dev, remember the Christmas when you took me on the sleigh ride?"

"Remember? How could I forget? That cop was such a prick. Arresting me for driving a horse and sleigh in the city without a proper license."

"I think that was because you scratched all those parked cars on that one street. That woman saw you and phoned the police."

"A bit of an overreaction, if you ask me."

She smiled, "It was the very first time I bailed you out."

"Not the last," I laughed.

"Probably best not to go there," she said.

"So tell me, how did you meet Austin?"

"Well, since you ask, it was at a party… a reception, actually. A number of investors I'd put together were celebrating a sale. I was there and, well, Austin just swept me off my feet, I guess." She suddenly had a far-away look in her eyes and a wide smile on her face. "He's been wonderful."

At that moment, the door to Mario's opened, and a figure with hair spiked in a variety of directions took two steps in and stood there, letting his eyes adjust. It felt like a wet blanket rolling across the room. I quickly grabbed Heidi's purse off the back of her stool and dropped it on the oak floor.

"Dev, what the hell are you doing?" she asked, then hopped off her stool and bent down to pick her purse up.

I draped my legs over her shoulders and held her below the bar. Austin looked around but didn't see her.

"Dev, Dev stop it," she laughed just as Austin walked around the corner of the bar and toward the two of us. I removed my legs, and Heidi stood up as Austin approached. "What the hell do you think you're doing, are you crazy?" Heidi laughed. "I'm not going to give you a—"

"What's going on here? Are you okay, honey?" Austin said, then physically pushed her behind him and glared at me.

"Austin, I, well, we were just talking. You remember Dev Haskell? He saw us the other night at Desmond's. He was the one who came over to congratulate us."

"I remember him, are you all right?" he asked, looking Heidi up and down. Then he brushed an imaginary something off her shoulder and turned toward me. "I'm not sure what your game is, but I'll not have Heidi involved."

"Relax, it was just a joke, I—"

"A joke? It certainly didn't look funny from where I stood. Come on, Heidi. We're leaving."

"Austin, I think—"

"You're leaving now."

"We were just talking, Dev and I are—"

"I know what the two of you were— now, move," he said and roughly pushed her toward the door.

I lost it and flew off my stool. The next thing I knew, Austin was on the floor, holding a bloody nose, and Heidi was yelling, "Dev, don't please, please."

"You, get out of here," the bartender yelled at me.

"Please, Dev, just leave."

Austin slowly got up off the floor, stepped behind Heidi then started to yell. "I've got witnesses; everyone here saw this maniac assault me. He tried to kill me. He—"

"Believe me, if I had tried, you'd already be dead."

"Just go, Dev, please? You're just making things worse."

"Get out of here, pal, before I call the cops," the bartender said.

"I've got your number, Haskell, do you hear? I've got your number. You'll rue the day you—"

"And I've got yours, Hackett. Does the name Bunny Hutch ring any bells? What about your ex-wives, Connie Adams, Marcia Paxton, or Nancy Reilly? One threatened to shoot you, and the other two fled the state."

"Come on, go, go, this man's insane," Hackett said, then took Heidi by the arm and hurried her out the door.

"I always thought a Navy Seal would be a little tougher," I called just as Heidi shot me a confused look.

"I'm calling the cops, buddy," the bartender said and picked up the phone.

Twenty-six

Louie shook his head. "Gee, amazing, the guy didn't want to hang around and get to know you better," he said then took a sip of his coffee. "Ugh."

"I just snapped. He shouted at Heidi, pushed her, and the next thing I knew, he was on the floor with a bloody nose, and Heidi was in-between the two of us."

"Well, I'd say you better prepare yourself for a pretty serious legal battle. He's liable to come after you saying you did everything from pull a gun on him to threatening everyone in the place."

"We were just talking. Why in the hell did he even show up?"

"Because he needs to maintain tight control, plus the fact that he might have an idea of the information you have about him. Of course, even if he didn't going in, he sure as hell knows about it now."

"So much for my casual, reasoned approach."

"Oh, that."

"She didn't go home last night, or if she did, it was close to sunrise. I was parked near her place until after four this morning, and she never turned up."

"Probably a good thing. I think under the circumstances, your actions could be construed as doing something other than attempting to be helpful."

"I just wanted to give her some accurate information so I—"

"At four in the damn morning? Dev, it's not a far leap to come to the conclusion you're stalking the poor woman."

"Me?"

"In the last twenty-four hours, you've broken into her home, shampooed her carpet, left flowers and a card on her kitchen table, forced her down on her knees between your legs in a bar, and assaulted her boyfriend. I'd say you'll be lucky if she doesn't file a restraining order against you."

"Heidi's not going to do that."

"Not unless Austin Hackett thinks it would be a good idea, and believe me, he won't stop there."

"God help him if he does."

"There, that's the spirit. That kind of comment will get everyone on your side, not. That's exactly the attitude he's hoping you'll display. You're playing right into his hands."

"But I—"

"No, I'm talking to you as your lawyer right now. You better tighten it up, pal, or you aren't going to have a snowball's chance in hell to help her. Oh, yeah, and even though he's a slime ball, a jerk like Austin Hackett will have you skinned alive in court."

"What am I supposed to do?"

"Nothing. At least nothing to that douche bag. What you can do is continue to find out everything possible about his activities, his business, his financial situation, and anyone *dealing* with him. Pending lawsuits, lawsuits already filed. You can…"

"Okay, I get it. It's just that he's such a putz."

"A putz who can make your life extremely difficult. Obviously, he's now aware you've been checking him out. After yelling that shit at him, he's more than aware."

"Good."

"Well, if the goal is to help Heidi, you may have just cut the time in half to accomplish that task."

Twenty-seven

Duly chastised by Louie, Morton and I set out to learn what we could about Austin Hackett. Our first stop was the Beaumont building, named after some guy named Beaumont, I guessed. It was a white-stone, multi-storied structure in the middle of a block of three-story brick buildings and left the distinct impression of someone giving you the finger. White marble with little waves of grey made up the floor and walls in the lobby of the place. The grey pattern in the marble gave me the impression of a hazardous chemical drifting across the water. The guard's desk, set just in front of the elevators, was constructed from the same marble and inhabited by three individuals in short-sleeve, white shirts, and blue trousers. The shirts had American flags stitched onto the right shoulders and shiny gold badges pinned onto the left breast pocket. The badges read Dustan Security.

"May I help you," one of the guys behind the counter asked.

"I'm looking for the offices of Austin Hackett."

One of the guards with his back to me turned, and half-whispered, "Getting sued?"

"Fortunately not. I just wanted to see about some representation." That caused all three to look up and study me for a long moment.

"Representation," the guy said as he picked up the phone, sounding like he didn't quite believe me. "Yes, I have a gentleman down here wishing to see about representation. Let me check. Do you have an appointment?"

"No, I don't. I was hoping I might just get some general information."

"He does not have an appointment. He's just looking for some general information. Okay, we'll send him up. Sixteenth floor, number sixteen-ten," the guy said, then gave a nod in the direction of the elevators.

I boarded the elevator with a middle-aged woman who stepped off on the ninth floor. Then I rode alone up to the sixteenth floor. The hallway was carpeted in an institutional grey carpet with a dark rubber baseboard and light grey walls. The trim around the doors was metal and painted the same color as the walls. The door to 1610 held a fogged glass panel with "Austin Hackett Attorney at Law" painted in black letters. I opened the door and entered a small reception area with comfortable looking chairs and a polished wood counter, maybe fifteen feet away. An attractive woman sat behind the counter, smiling.

"May I help you?"

"Hi, I was just stopping by. I wanted to see about getting some general information, in case I need representation."

She held her pasted on smile like this was an everyday occurrence, then reached down to a cardboard box along the side of the counter and pulled out two brochures, exactly the same. She was still smiling when she sat up. "Hopefully, this will answer your questions and maybe prompt some others."

I glanced over her shoulder into what appeared to be a conference room. The drapes had been pulled, though not completely, and I could see spiked haired Austin Hackett sitting with his back toward me. Opposite him sat a middle-aged couple holding hands. The woman looked about ready to break into tears. The guy looked ready to kill. Someone to the left of them was moving his hands back and forth, I guessed as he spoke, although I couldn't see much beyond his wrists. Hackett sat there, shaking his head 'no' in response to whatever was being said.

"Will there be anything else, sir?"

"No, thank you. You've been quite helpful," I said, then left the office and took the elevator down to the ground floor.

"Everything go okay?" the security guy who joked about being sued asked.

I held up the two brochures and headed out the revolving door.

I waited outside for almost forty-five minutes before the couple I'd seen in Hackett's office walked out of the building. They shook hands with a guy in a blue suit and had a word or two before he headed down the street in the opposite direction. Then they turned and walked toward me.

"Excuse me," I said as they approached.

"Believe me, we don't have any money," the guy said.

"Certainly not now," the woman added as he steered her around me.

"Could I just take a moment of your time, I—"

"Hey, look, pal, we've—"

"It's about Austin Hackett."

"Hackett?" he said, and they both stopped.

"I saw you up in his office. It didn't look like things were exactly going your way. I'm a private investigator, my name is Devlin Haskell, and I'm investigating Austin Hackett."

"You oughta just shoot the bastard."

"Tom, don't. Investigating him for what?" the woman asked.

"That's kind of complicated. I'd gladly buy you lunch or coffee or a drink if you'd like to talk. You can leave at any time. I'm just trying to get as much information on him as I can."

"What the hell were you doing up in his office if you're trying to get information?" the guy asked.

"Getting these," I said and held up the brochures Hackett's receptionist had given me.

"Tom?"

"Okay, yeah, sure. I could use a drink, a strong drink, but the Starbucks around the corner might be a better idea. What'd you say your name was?"

"Haskell, Devlin Haskell, I go by Dev."

"Tom Connelly, Dev, this is my wife Jean," he said, extending his hand.

Over coffee, the Connelly's told me they owned a specialty food shop. "The store is just a front, so to speak. Our real business used to be direct mail. You know, catalogs. But now, all that's pretty much been transferred to online. We're up twenty-eight percent this year over last and just hired a fourth person to take over our shipping and warehouse. Then this shit happened."

"So if it's online, what's Hackett's deal?"

"It's the online that we figure got his interest. Not the business as such, but our success. We were written up in the paper, what two months ago, Jeanie?"

"Closer to four now. We're one of the top twenty small companies in the state. Once that article appeared, it wasn't long before Mr. Hackett's firm hit us with a lawsuit. Failure to comply…"

"With the ADA," I said.

"Yeah, even though we've been grandfathered in. How'd you know? Our attorney told us by the time we battle this out in court, it's liable to run us at least ten grand. The suit he filed hits us for over a hundred grand in updates and improvements. The bastard said we have to put an elevator in. For God's sake, it's a two-story building, and it's all offices on the second floor. I think we'll just close the store, take the hit, and hope we survive."

"We will survive," Jean said. "And then we'll redouble our efforts online."

"Your case sounds similar to others I've heard about. Has he offered to settle out of court?"

"No, in fact, today's meeting was to tell us he's actually going to file suit for over a hundred grand. I mean, Jesus Christ. We got a one-inch lip on the door and some guy with a walker trips on it, and now we're gonna be out of business. My ma uses a walker, goddamnit."

"Tom, you're raising your voice, again," Jean said and placed her hand over her husbands in an effort to calm him.

"Well, Jesus, it's enough to really piss me off."

"Your situation sounds similar to some other cases I'm aware of with this guy. I can tell you this. After he files, he'll most likely come back and offer to settle out of court for five to eight grand, depending. That said, the few folks that have stuck to their guns and fought him in the past usually end up having their cases dropped, but they've probably spent that same amount of money in legal fees."

"So, what's he get out of it?"

"The money. Rather then you spending the funds to make the improvements, he takes the money, and well, keeps it."

"Can he do that? That's gotta be against the law."

"He settles out of court with folks. They basically pay him, and he just keeps the money."

"Now, I really want you to shoot the bastard."

"Expect him to come to you sometime in the near future with an offer to settle."

They both sat there and shook their heads.

"Before this, his scam was in the porn industry."

"Pornography?" This time Jean raised her voice.

"Yeah." I went on to explain the Bunny Hutch scam.

"So what's your interest in all this? Did he sue you?"

"No, mine's more personal." I took out a business card and wrote down Pat O'Leary and Jack Griffith's names. "These are two attorneys who fought this jerk and won. They could probably turn you on to other folks as well. I might also recommend that you file a complaint with the state bar association. I know they're looking into this guy. I've heard talk of disbarment, and your complaint just may serve as one more nail in his coffin."

"I'll file the complaint this afternoon."

"You got my card. Please keep me posted."

"Yeah, you bet. Listen, same thing. You hear something you let us know. Here's my card," Tom said and slid his card across the table.

Twenty-eight

Morton and I had just walked into the office after my meeting with the Connelly's. It was the middle of the afternoon and at least two hours before the girls in the third-floor apartment were due home from work. Louie was seated in my desk chair, looking out the window with the binoculars. "You picking up some action across the street?"

"No, just some big guy parked out there in that green SUV. He's been sitting there for the last couple of hours. I thought he might be dead, but every once in a while, he moves."

"Let me take a look." Louie handed me the binoculars. I adjusted the knob and focused in on the guy. He was sitting in a dark green SUV, a Mercury Mountaineer, to be exact. From the look of the rust over the wheel wells, not the newest vehicle in the fleet. I'd done enough stakeouts in my day to recognize that the angle his side mirror was turned wouldn't help his driving. "I'd guess that guy is checking something or someone out. That side mirror looks like it's focused on the entrance to our building."

"You think he's checking Gary?"

"The State Farm guy? Gotta be an easier way to get better rates than that. No, I'd say he's checking us out, or me to be more precise."

"Hackett?"

"Yeah, that putz is probably working for him after my interaction with Hackett last night. No offense, but if you spotted him, I'm guessing he can't be too experienced."

"No offense taken. What do you want to do?"

"Do? Nothing, I think we'll just let him sit there, waste the day, and hopefully run up the bill Hackett will have to pay."

I made a bunch of phone calls, left two messages for Heidi, and one for AJ. Louie tapped away on his keyboard. It was close to six when I glanced out the window again. The SUV with our pal sitting in it was gone. "Hey, your pal left."

Louie looked up from his computer, "He's pulling away now?"

"No, I just checked, and he's gone. No idea when he actually left."

"Maybe he had to hit the head."

"If he had any brains, he'd just walk into The Spot. No one's going to say anything to him."

"Speaking of which I'm almost at a stopping point. You up for one?"

"I could be talked into it. Fifteen minutes?"

"I'll see you over there," Louie said and proceeded to shut down his computer.

I'd lost track of how long we'd been at the bar. It was still light out when I walked in, and it had been dark now for quite a while. The place was quiet tonight, just one couple in a booth behind us, two guys at the far end of the bar, and three girls throwing darts. The blonde in the trio was pretty loud. She seemed to be more than a little over-served and looked familiar, although I couldn't place her.

Jimmy stepped in front of us, "You guys ready for another, or you gonna call it a night?"

Louie looked over at me and raised his eyebrows. "Maybe just one more?"

"Yeah, why not."

Jimmy delivered the drinks in record time, then walked down toward the two guys seated at the end. Louie and I had both worked at avoiding any discussion that had to do with Austin Hackett.

"So, what's your plan for tomorrow?"

"I'm going to continue lining up folks who will help me convince Heidi that Hackett's a jerk."

"Think she'll buy into it?"

"I can only try. I've got his ex-wives. Nancy Reilly is the only one locally, but she's credible. Maybe the couple I spoke with today, the Connelly's. I was thinking Clarence Rutherford, the limo guy, but he'll probably stick to that client confidentiality crap, so I'll consider him my "B" team along with those attorneys whose names you gave me."

"Griffith and O'Leary?"

"Yeah. Time is running out. I can feel it. I've got two calls into Heidi, and she hasn't returned them. It might be a coincidence, but it's very unlike her. Even in the past, when she was pissed off, she'd still take my call if only to give me a piece of her mind. I'd say he's putting pressure on her."

"Maybe he's gonna sue, and he told her the best thing she could do would be to not correspond with you. Frankly, that could be some sound legal advice, at least from her perspective."

"And his."

"Well, yeah." Louie drained his drink, then pushed off his stool. "I gotta head home. Don't do anything stupid tonight."

"How much trouble can I get in on the way home?"

He didn't answer that, but just gave me a look and said, "See you in the morning."

Twenty-nine

The gals throwing darts had cleared out along with the couple in the booth behind me. I was retelling jokes with Jimmy and ordered another beer. The two guys at the end of the bar seemed to be mesmerized with whoever Jimmy Fallon was interviewing on The Tonight Show. Jimmy, the bartender, was busy telling me about his daughter finishing medical school.

"Good thing she got her brains from her mom," I said and drained my glass.

"And her good looks," Jimmy added.

"Probably see you tomorrow, Jimmy. Take care."

I headed out to my car, it was parked on Victoria, back toward the rear of my building. The stoplight on the corner had just turned red, but at this hour, it was quiet, not a moving vehicle in sight in any direction. I crossed the intersection at a diagonal and headed for my car. I gave a little whistle once I crossed the street, and Morton popped his head up in the backseat. He held what was left of his chew toy in his mouth.

"Hey, Morton."

He began pacing back and forth across the rear seat, then he suddenly dropped his chew toy and started barking. Just as I began to turn round something smashed into the side of my head, knocking me to the ground. I saw a momentary flash of stars but was still conscious enough to half somersault back onto my feet.

It was the two guys from The Spot, the ones who'd been drinking at the end of the bar. It suddenly dawned on me that the larger of the two was the same guy we'd spotted sitting in the Mercury Mountaineer earlier in the day. I recognized the crew cut, not that it did much for his looks.

"Thought we'd maybe relay a little message to you, asshole. One you're not going to forget." He appeared much larger in person, standing in the street and looking to hurt me. He had the build of a weightlifter, muscled chest, arms, and a thick neck. There was a barbed wire design tattooed around his left bicep, and his nose seemed to flatten into his cheeks like it had been broken so many times it was just cosmetic. I picked up an accent, maybe the south side of Chicago. "Think you're some kind of tough guy playing games in a bar with our pal's piece of ass?"

"You mean those girls playing darts?"

"Shut up," he said. They suddenly spread a little further apart, half turned sideways with their fists up, and got in a half crouched position. I took a couple of steps back then bumped into the trunk of my car. Morton's barking had gone up a notch or two, and he didn't sound very happy.

"Can't we talk this over? Come on."

His pal pulled what looked like a black leather sap from out of his back pocket, slapped it in the palm of his hand, and grinned. The musclebound creep with the tattoo said, "You're about to get your ass kicked, dumb shit. Even your stupid dog knows."

"What'd you just say?"

"I said your stupid dog knows…"

He suddenly shut-up at the sound of the hammer clicking on my .38. As I drew it out from behind my back, they gave one another a quick glance, not exactly sure what to do next. I kept the weapon pointed down, letting it hang alongside my knee.

"You think you're gonna shoot us? We supposed to be scared now? Cops'll lock your ass up and throw away the damn key," he said, then took a half step back.

"Not when they see who I shot. Maybe you should just get your ass out of here before you get hurt, both of you."

"You ain't getting off that easy, dumb shit."

"You know, there always seems to be someone just stupid enough to think I'm not serious. I don't know what it is about me."

"Maybe it's because you're an asshole."

"Probably," I said and fired my pistol into his right foot from a distance of about three feet.

"Arghhh," he screamed as he went down, grabbing his foot and rolling into the middle of the street. There seemed to be a halfway decent-sized hole in the sole of his shoe.

His partner had a stunned look on his face. Just as he began to refocus on me, I slammed the barrel of the .38 across the bridge of his nose. When he brought both hands up to his face, I kicked him between the legs, definitely making contact. He groaned and stumbled against the trunk of my car. I grabbed him by the hair and slammed his head against the trunk a few times, making a hollow thunk sound and denting my car until he went limp and just slid to the ground.

The yellow glare from the street light on the far corner gave a macabre look to the entire scene. I stepped over to the guy lying in the middle of the street, holding his foot. His groan suddenly turned into more of a whimper, and his eyes grew wide as I placed the barrel of the .38 on the tip of his nose and pressed hard. I pressed my knee up against his chest and pinned him to the asphalt. "I'm thinking it might be a good idea if you two just went back to whatever shithole you came from, don't you?"

The look of fear on his face was palpable, and he half nodded then gave a whispered, "Yes, sir."

I stood up, got in my car, and drove off, leaving the two of them lying in the street. I spotted the Mercury Mountaineer on a side street about a block away from The Spot. I pulled over, got out, and jammed a screwdriver into all four tires then drove home.

Thirty

I was in the process of checking out the women gathered at the bus stop, then moving the binoculars back to the girls across the street in the apartment. One of the apartment girls was wrapped in some dreadful looking brown bathrobe thing and sipping from what looked like a can of Seven-Up. She looked an awful lot like the drunk blonde throwing darts in The Spot the night before. Unfortunately for me, her roommate was dressed and in the process of waving good-bye.

"Anything shaking?" Louie asked as he came through the door and tossed his laptop on the picnic table.

"Nothing worthwhile."

"I trust you made it home okay."

"Me? Yeah sure, no problems."

"Someone rear-end your car? Your trunk has a bunch of dents."

"Tree branch from the storm a while back."

Morton was happily attacking the new chew toy we picked up on the way into the office. His reward for try-

ing to alert me last night. Louie gave him a good rub behind the ears, but Morton was too engaged to pay him
much attention.

"He really likes those things," Louie said, then
winced as he tasted the coffee.

"Yeah, I guess we left it on overnight, again. I didn't
have the courage to try some this morning."

"Nor the brains to make a fresh pot."

"That too." My phone rang at just that moment.
"Haskell investigations."

"Hi, Dev, AJ."

"Hey, how's it going? You recovered?"

"Yeah, back to normal, whatever that is," she said,
and chuckled. "Just wanted to let you know I'd survived
our last encounter."

There was a long pause before I picked up the slack.
"Good, good. You feel like risking one more get together?"

"I suppose. I will if you will." I wasn't sure, but I
thought I sensed a degree of hesitation in her voice.

"AJ, you almost make it sound like a dare like we're
jumping off a cliff or something."

"Maybe not far from the truth."

"Would you be up for another try at dinner? I'll let
you order for me so I won't contaminate you?" I said.

"You don't have to do that."

"You busy tonight?"

"Well, actually no, now that you mention it. Would that work for you? I mean, I wasn't calling just so you'd ask me out. It was more of a funny…"

"Hey, if you can make it tonight, I'll pick you up at seven. Your job is to pick the restaurant. Anywhere you like, it doesn't matter to me. I'll have fun just being with you."

"Oh, thank you."

"See you at seven?"

"Well yeah, I'm looking forward to it, Dev, honest." I wasn't quite sure how promising that was, but I'd take it.

"She's going out with you again, AJ?" Louie asked.

"Yeah, you heard it. Dinner tonight, she picks the restaurant."

"Poor woman seems to be a glutton for punishment."

"What can go wrong?"

"Don't even go there," Louie said.

"Check this out, talk about covering all the bases," I said then dialed the phone. "Clarence, please. Hi, Clarence, this is Dev Haskell. I met you at the Subway that night you were— Yeah right. Listen, I was hoping I could hire one of your limos for the evening. No, nothing like that, just trying to impress a woman. Just pick us up for dinner and drive us home. Well, I was planning on picking her up at seven. No, I don't know, she's picking the place. It'll be somewhere in town. Great, about a quarter to seven? Let me give you my address." I hung up the phone and looked across at Louie. "There, satisfied? I'm not taking any chances this time."

"I hope you know what you're doing."

"That's always been the question, hasn't it?"

I placed three more phone calls to Heidi over the course of the day, one to her home, one to her office, and one to her cell. If she was anywhere near a phone, there was no way she could say she missed all three calls. I still didn't hear from her. I left the office at five and begged off stopping for a quick one at The Spot with Louie, knowing how that was bound to turn out.

I took Morton for a nice long walk, got him settled in for the night, then proceeded to get ready. I figured if AJ was choosing the restaurant, it was going to be someplace fairly fancy. So I got out a suit and a white shirt just back from the dry cleaners. I had a half dozen ties, but three of them were Christmas ties that when you squeezed them, they lit up, another one just played jingle bells. Of the other two, one was adult-oriented, the male organ if that translates, that was out and then a pink tie that went with my grey suit. Maybe. Anyway, that was it, a grey suit, white shirt, and a pink tie. The limo driver rang my doorbell about five minutes early.

"Mr. Haskell," he said when I opened the door.

"Yeah, please call me Dev. Nice to meet you."

"Richie DeVon," he said, extending a hand. He was dressed the way Clarence had been the other night, a dark suit coat with epaulets on the shoulders and a black cap with a shiny, patent leather visor. "Please, just call me Richie. Clarence said I'm supposed to give you the deluxe treatment."

"You just get me to and from this dinner without me screwing it up, and that'll be deluxe enough for me."

"I think I can do that. I'm a few minutes early. We can leave if you'd like or if you want to wait, that's fine, too. It's all up to you."

"Tell you what, let's go. We can stop at the flower store. There's one just up the block. I want to grab some flowers and hopefully fool this woman into thinking I'm a genuinely nice guy."

I picked up a nice bouquet of a half dozen yellow roses, fragrant ones at that. As I climbed back in the limo, Richie said, "You aren't taking any chances, are you? Either that or you're really in the dog house."

"Actually, both those statements are pretty accurate. I'd tell you, but I'm not even sure I believe everything that's happened trying to date this girl. She lives over on Collette Place, just off Dorothea. You know where that is?"

"I do indeed. Now you just sit back and smell the roses Dev, and I'll have you there in about ten minutes."

Thirty-one

You know, it's amazing. I've lived in this town pretty much all my life except for some time in the Army. But the things you see when you're not driving when you actually have time to look and stare— houses and shrubs and well, just everything. The trip to AJ's passed almost too quickly.

"That's it right down there, the brick front with the hedge," I said.

Richie pulled over right in front of AJ's and stopped. "Okay, now Dev, do you know if you're going to hang here for a drink or take off right away?"

"Actually, I don't know. It's kind of up to her, I guess."

"No problem. I'll just keep my eye on the door. When you leave if you could just linger by her front door for a few seconds to give me enough time to jump out and hold the limo door open for the two of you."

"Done. I like the way you're thinking, Richie," I said, then patted him on the shoulder before I stepped out of the limo.

I rang her doorbell and hid the roses behind my back. AJ answered the door a moment later. She was wearing sparkling sandals, tight-fitting jeans, and bursting out of a pink tube top that looked like it was a couple of sizes too small. I wanted to keep her all to myself and ravage her.

"Dev?" she said, then got this funny smirk on her face. "Oh, my God! Look at you. You're all dressed up."

I pulled the bouquet of roses from behind my back and handed them to her.

"Oh, Jesus, you're kidding? I haven't gotten flowers from anyone for, well, since forever. That's so nice of you. Oh, sorry, come on in. It's going to take me a while to change, but if you can just be patient I'll slip into something—"

"No, don't, please. I mean, you look beautiful. I love the outfit. Really I'd love to just lock the door and keep you to myself, to be honest."

"Here, come on in. Let me put these in some water," she said, then hurried through her living room and into the kitchen.

I gave Richie the thumbs up, stepped inside, closed the door, then hurried back to the kitchen. Lady Godiva was lying in a basket. Her tail started wagging and thumping against the ceramic tile floor as soon as I entered the kitchen, but she stayed where she was.

"Give her a little rub behind the ears, will you Dev? Just so she knows she's loved," AJ said, then opened a cabinet door, pulled out a vase, and set it on the granite countertop. The kitchen cabinets were white with brass handles and offset by the shiny black granite countertop.

The windows along the back wall overlooked a rose garden edged with a neatly trimmed boxwood hedge. There wasn't a weed in sight.

"There," she said, trimming the last of the rose stems and then setting the bouquet into the cut-glass vase. "Gorgeous, and oh the scent. Dev, how did you know I was partial to roses?"

"Guys like me just know these sorts of things."

She either accepted that comment or dismissed it, I wasn't sure which. "Here, let me slip into something a little more in keeping with your outfit."

"No, please, don't AJ. You look beautiful."

"Oh, thank you. But you're all dressed up, and well, I've got my come fuck me sandals on, and…"

"They're perfect. Where did you decide we'd go?"

"Well, to tell you the truth, I was thinking Shamrock's. After the last couple of disasters, I kind of figured you were more of a cheeseburger and beer guy, so I thought we'd just keep it simple."

"Sounds perfect to me. I want to ditch this tie anyway, and I can leave my suit coat in the car."

"You sure? I mean, it'll just take a second to change."

No woman has ever changed in just a second. At the mere mention of cheeseburgers and beer, my stomach had started growling, and besides, AJ was really gorgeous, and there was always the hope she'd follow the intent of those sparkly sandals she was wearing.

"Just stay exactly the way you are, and let's go have a fun night, okay?"

"You talked me into it," she said.

Thirty-two

I started undoing my tie the moment I stepped out of the front door. I fiddled with it on the front stoop for a moment while AJ locked the door, giving Richie just enough time to run around the front of the limo and open the door for us. AJ seemed oblivious. "Where did you park?"

"Your carriage awaits, madam."

"Huh? A limo, you got a limo? Are you kidding? I, I don't know what to say."

"Maybe just hop in, and we can talk on the way," I said.

"Oh this is going to be so special, I can't believe I'm… Oh. My. God! Richie? Richie DeVon, is that really you? I don't believe it; it can't be! Dev how did you know?" she screamed, then jumped up into Richie's arms, wrapped her legs around his waist, and gave him a big hug. She unwrapped herself, stepped back, grabbed his face in both her hands, and planted a big long kiss right on his lips. "Oh, it's been so long."

Richie had now gotten more action than I had with AJ. He looked just as shocked as me. "AJ, what the… I thought you were out east somewhere. Maryland or someplace?"

"No, actually, Marietta. Marietta, Georgia. I was doing financial work, and well, an opportunity developed back here, and I went for it thinking I didn't have a chance. They gave the job to someone else, but he broke a leg skiing or something, and so, here I am. Oh, my God! I just can't believe it's you." She turned to look at me, eyes wide and all aglow. "Richie took me to homecoming our senior year in high school, Dev."

"And Christmas formal and the Spring Fling," Richie said, suddenly all smiles.

"Don't forget the Graduation Ball, remember? Naughty, naughty," AJ said, then elbowed Richie and gave an evil grin.

"Oh, ahem, well yeah. Anyway, we knew one another in high school," Richie said.

AJ slinked up next to him and stroked his hand with her index finger while she smiled at me.

"Great, and neither one of you knew the other was in town?" I said.

"You ever finish college?" AJ asked.

"Yep, got one more year left in law school. I'm going on the GI bill."

"Really? Oh, I'm so proud of you. You always said you wanted to practice law, even when we were kids."

"So, should we head down to Shamrock's?" I said. I felt whatever passion there had been in the night had pretty much just evaporated, at least in my case.

"Oh yeah, Shamrock's, sure, here," Richie said and grabbed hold of the passenger door again.

"Yeah, I suppose," AJ said, sounding a little disappointed.

"Tell you what, I'd like to just look at the scenery. If it's okay, why doesn't AJ ride in the front so the two of you can kind of get caught up?"

"Oh no, Dev, I couldn't do that," AJ said. "Well, I mean, unless you really wouldn't mind, then I suppose we could."

"Not a problem," I said as AJ opened the door to the limo and quickly slid into the front passenger seat.

Richie looked at me and shrugged as I climbed into the back. "Sorry, man," he whispered.

"Actually, Richie, I should have seen it coming. Not to worry, I get it."

"You sure, man?"

"Yeah."

Once Richie climbed behind the wheel and started the car, I pulled out my phone and pretended to answer it. "Hello? Speaking. Now, tonight? I suppose, give me thirty minutes, and I'll be there," I said, then put the phone back in my pocket. "Hey, guys change of plans, I've got an injured client. Would it be alright if you ran me home, Richie? Sorry AJ, but business calls."

"You sure?" she said, suddenly looking hopeful.

I caught Richie looking at me funny in the rearview mirror.

"Yeah, sorry, but I have to attend to my client."

"You can get to Dev's house faster if you take 35E," AJ said.

Thirty-three

As Louie stepped into the office the following morning, he said, "So?"

"Relax, I made a fresh pot, and there's still some left."

"Not the coffee, meathead, although thanks. I could use some. I meant the star-studded night, a limo, dinner, no holds barred. Hopefully, your evening ended with fireworks. Yes?"

"To be specific, no, not even close. I think I was with her for a total of about eighteen minutes."

"Eighteen minutes? What the hell did you do this time?"

"Nothing, other than hire a limo driver she apparently had a previous relationship with." I went on to tell Louie about my night.

"So, what did you end up doing?"

"Morton and I watched a movie, and we were both asleep by about 10:30."

"I'm going to have to find someone else to live through vicariously. This just isn't working," Louie said.

A little bell suddenly went off on my computer, signaling an incoming message. I clicked the image in my toolbar for email. "Oh, here we go. Apologies from AJ, coming across the line as we speak," I said then opened her email.

"An apology? What does it say?"

I just sat and stared at the message. The image was a large black door on the front of a structure that looked about five hundred years old with an open window above the door. A ray of sunshine was streaming through the window with some kind of white dove that looked like it was about to fly in.

"Come on, what's it say, Dev?"

"God never closes a door without opening a window."

"What the hell does that mean?"

I thought for a long moment, then said, "It could mean a number of things. I'll take it to mean she and Richie reconnected last night."

"Reconnected?"

"I'm guessing they both got more action than I've had in the last five dates."

"Oh, sorry, man."

"It was doomed from the start. One of those things that probably was just never meant to happen."

"Now don't you be going all philosophical on me."

"Far from it, just funny is all, you know…" my phone rang. "Haskell Investigations."

"Is this Dev?"

"It is."

"Hi, Dev, this is Richie DeVon, from last night."

"Hi, Richie," I said and looked at the image on my computer screen again. "Things work out for you and AJ?"

"Better than expected, actually. That's kinda why I'm calling. I wanted to tell you thanks, and I hope you didn't think I was trying to cut into your plans or anything. It just, you know, happened."

"Yeah, don't worry, not a problem on this end."

"It was just so crazy. I mean, we dated in high school, but something always seemed to go wrong. I cracked up my dad's car one time with AJ. Another time she was wearing some outfit of her sister's, and it got ripped. One time we tried to sneak some wine from her folk's house and ended up spilling it on her mom's new carpet. It was almost like things were destined to fail every time we got together."

"Believe me, I can identify with all of that," I said.

"Well anyway, I just wanted to say thanks for being so understanding. It's really nice of you. I'm guessing you faked that call about the injured client last night."

"Well, it was either that or I'd have to listen to how wonderful you were in high school, and wasn't it just funny that you met again and isn't it a small town all the way through my dinner. I'm happy for both of you."

"Yeah, sorry about that. Hopefully, the night wasn't a total bust on your end."

"Are you kidding, I just called this red-headed gal I know, and we made a night of it. Glad you guys were able to connect."

"Well, if it's any consolation you're not paying for last night. I spoke to Clarence this morning, and he already reversed your credit card charge. So thanks, man. I owe you, big time."

"Thanks for that, Richie, I appreciate the effort. Hey, can I ask you a question, maybe off the record?"

"Sure?"

"I was talking to Clarence the other day. I'll be honest. He didn't give me much info. He's pretty guarded about his clients, and I get that. There's just this one guy I wanted to find out about. At one time, he had three or four guys brought up to a lake place with this woman and…"

Richie half-laughed, "You're not talking about that stripper named Pepper, are you?"

"As a matter of fact, that's exactly who I'm talking about. Actually, I learned about the event from her, from Pepper. She was a client of mine some years back, working under a different name."

"I had to drive them all up there and pick them up a few days later. As a matter of fact, they tossed her in the trunk on the way up. I was afraid I'd lose my license with guys drinking and partying in the back of the limo. It was pretty crazy, course they ended up tipping pretty well, too. Then a few days later, I had to drive up there and bring everyone back to town. Thankfully, they were all exhausted on the ride back."

"You remember where you took them?"

"Up north, if memory serves. I mean, I think I could get there again, if I had to. But I couldn't give you exact directions. I'm trying to think of the client's name. I've picked up a couple of folks at the airport for him and, Hackman, Heckle—"

"Hackett? Austin Hackett?"

"Yeah, that's the one. Some big money guy, although just between you and me, there always seems to be something kind of not quite right with him."

"How so?"

"Nothing I can put my finger on. Just, oh comments I've picked up from folks while I'm driving. With the exception of that group going up to his lake place with Pepper in the trunk, there doesn't seem to be a lot of love lost between him and the passengers I've had."

"You said it was his lake place you drove to?"

"Oh yeah, quite the spread, too. Big cabin, lots of rooms. I remember because I had to carry everyone's luggage into their rooms. It was five folks, four guys and then that Pepper chick, and everyone had their own private room with a bath attached. I remember there was even a pool in the back overlooking the lake if you can believe it."

"I can."

"Hey, I've gotta run. I have to try and stay awake for the next two hours in a tort reform class. I really appreciate you being so understanding, Dev. Last night just, well, it just happened, and I don't think AJ or I could have changed it, even if we'd wanted to. I don't know. I guess it was written in the stars or something."

"I appreciate the call, Richie. Thanks for thinking of me."

"Let me know if I can ever help you, Dev."

"Thanks, I'll keep that in mind," I said, and then we hung up.

"So?" Louie said.

"Great, not only does she drop me for this guy, but he turns out to be really nice."

"And he knew Hackett?"

"Yeah, he's the driver that ran Swindle Lawless, aka Pepper, up to that lake place with four guys. What I didn't know was that Hackett owns the lake place."

Something seemed to catch Louie's eye out on the street. "Hey, check that out," he said.

I turned to look just as the light on the corner changed, and a tow truck with a green Mercury Mountaineer mounted on the bed and sporting four flat tires drove down the street.

"You think that was the same car that guy was driving the other day, the one that was parked across the street?"

"Can't really say. I guess I wasn't paying that close attention."

Thirty-four

My phone conversation with Richie got me thinking about Clarence's comment the other day. How Hackett had a fancy place with a wrought-iron fence, a big gate, and a security system. I thought it might be worth a look. I Googled Hackett and had his address in under two minutes. It was close to noon when I drove past. I could say I was just checking out his house, but the term house wouldn't do the place justice, it was a mansion.

A gorgeous mansion that looked like something out of a movie. A large, red-brick colonial with a slate roof, white trim, and stained glass windows. A circular drive wound around large oak trees in front of the place before it emptied out into the street through a set of wrought-iron double gates. The fence around the place was wrought-iron, about eight feet high strung between massive brick pillars ten to twelve feet apart. As I drove past, automatic sprinklers were in the process of watering the well-kept lawn. A silver Jaguar was parked up next to the front door and just behind that sat a red BMW that looked an awful lot like Heidi's.

I drove past every half-hour, virtually on the dot. The last time I drove past, Heidi's car was gone, so I headed back to my office. I had a message waiting on my phone when I returned. The caller ID came up as unknown, although Heidi identified herself and said she was returning my call. She would have been more accurate if she'd said she was returning my numerous calls to her cell, her home, and her office, but I was so glad just to hear her voice I wasn't about to complain.

"Hi Dev, returning your call," she'd said and then hung up, like she'd just stepped out for a quick lunch or something instead of waiting for a day-and-a-half to get back to me using some 'unknown' phone. Probably a payphone, which suggested to me that Hackett was monitoring all her calls. There was only one thing to do.

* * *

"Dev?" Heidi said, stepping out of her office once the receptionist had announced my presence.

"Hi, sorry to interrupt your day. I was wondering if I could take just a minute of your time."

The receptionist shot Heidi a quick glance. I was sure the woman chalked me up to be Heidi's sometime loser boyfriend who just wouldn't go away now that things were so wonderful in Heidi's love life.

"Yeah, sure, I can spare a minute, I guess. But not much more. Come on in," she said, then held the door for me as I entered her office. "Hold my calls, Kate," she said and closed the door behind me as soon as I entered. I sat down in one of the plush black leather chairs in front of her massive desk and made a mental note of the dozen pink roses in the vase on her credenza. Heidi stood, crossed her arms, and leaned back ever so slightly against her desk, suggesting she really wasn't going to give me more than a minute. It felt like I was back in the principal's office.

"So what did you want, Dev?" she asked, not sounding all that happy.

"I just wanted to apologize for the way things turned out the other…"

"Turned out? You mean when you forced me to my knees and made it look like I was going to go down on you? When you assaulted Austin in the bar? Or did you just mean when you threatened to kill him? I could go on."

"Look, would you just calm down for a minute? I can explain, I think."

"Oh, please do," she said, glaring and drawing her arms closer together, which caused her breasts to rise. I guess maybe she caught my not-so-quick glance. "God, you are so damn predictable. Such a stupid one-track mind. Do you have any idea of the damage you've done?"

"I said I was sorry."

"Sorry?" she half screamed, then looked around, grabbed a file from her desk, and threw it at me. "Oh! you, you absolute idiot."

"I just lost it when he pushed you. I saw him shove you and it was like he hit you and, I don't know what happened, I don't even remember slapping him."

She stormed around her desk, sat down in the high back leather office chair then spun round to face me. "Slapping him? Is that what you call it? You punched him three times, Dev. I was afraid you were going to kill him."

I gave a little shrug and nodded at her last comment, which fortunately seemed to take the wind out of her sails. She's always been a bit like me. If she's bitching and yelling, she'll get it over with and then steam. Unfortunately, with me, that takes a minute or two, with Heidi, we're talking a couple of days. And if she's not yelling, but just seething, best to stay away for at least a week.

"Oh, Dev, honey, we've had a lot of fun. And, I hope I've been as good to you as you've been to me, but sometimes we change. As much as I love the incorrigible teenager you still are, I think I've found something, someone, who is better for me. I need something more than crazy parties, waking up with whipped cream all over me, or my clothes scattered out in the front yard."

"Look, Heidi, I've lost count of the broken hearts you've had, but I've always been there to pick up the pieces. I can't count the number of goofballs you thought were finally THE guy you were meant to spend the rest of your life with."

"But, Austin is different."

"I'll say."

"Now, Dev…"

"Heidi, he's lied to you, a lot, just for starters. And…"

"Oh," she said, shaking her head. There was a sharp edge to her tone. "Lied? that is really rich coming from you."

"This isn't about me. This is about someone making a huge damn mistake. This is about you buying into this guy's bullshit."

"Well, you'd certainly be the one with knowledge about bullshit."

"Heidi, listen to me. Did you know that he's been married three times before? That he drained the bank accounts of all three women. He abused them, assaulted them, tied them up in the damn basement for Christ's sake. Are you aware that…"

"Get out, Dev, just get out. I don't want to hear any more of this nonsense from you. Get out of my office."

"Heidi, he's going to be disbarred. The state is looking at him because…"

"Because he's fighting every day for disabled Americans, some of whom, for your information, are veterans, probably friends of yours. People who've been injured or maybe born into a situation that makes life unfair and Austin is one of the few people standing up for them. Every day he puts himself on the line for folks, who, through no fault of their own, are disadvantaged, and he—"

"Heidi, that's bullshit. He's scamming folks. I've talked to some of them and—"

"You've talked to them?" her voice was suddenly very quiet. If there was any ice left to stand on, it had just become too thin. "You talked to them?"

"I've talked to a couple of attorneys, some folks who have been sued by him. Some people who pretended to be injured, and then when he settled out of court, he screwed them and wouldn't live up to the bargain he'd made. Yeah, Heidi, I've spoken to one of his former wives. She carries a gun now she's so afraid of him. She has a restraining order out there against him. The other two just fled the state. After he drained their bank accounts and, in one case, spent their inheritance, they decided they'd rather live anywhere else rather than be near that nut case."

"I don't believe it."

"Ask him."

"You, you think, because of our past history, you can come in here and spread these kinds of lies? Dev, I'm sorry, but I expected better, even from someone like you. You know, let me tell you something. I promised I would never let you know this, but I think you should."

"So, tell me."

"Virtually all my girlfriends have asked me at one time or another why I was with you. Why I let you near me, why I slept with you, bailed you out, lent you money."

"I always paid you back."

"Oh Dev, that's not the point. You're in here sounding like, like a fifteen-year-old little boy making up fantastic tales. I suppose all the articles about him are wrong, my mistake, he doesn't stand up for the rights of those less fortunate, Dev. No, he should be down with you at The Spot bar every night, talking about all he's going to accomplish and then never doing a thing about it."

"Heidi, if you'd just give me a minute to explain. This guy is—"

"Your time is up Dev. You need to leave.

"Heidi, I—"

"Leave."

"But I—"

"Leave now, or I'm calling security."

Thirty-five

Morton and I were sharing another beer. He'd eaten one of the tacos I'd grabbed for dinner, not that I really cared. My so-called talk with Heidi was like pulling a black cloud over me. AJ falling head over heels for Richie hadn't helped any, either. I was lying on the couch in my den, watching some tear-jerker about a young mom who'd been given just four weeks to live. It wasn't doing much to help my mental state at the moment, so I turned off the TV and went to bed.

Morton woke me a little before four the following morning. He was sitting up in bed, growling. A low growl, the kind he seemed to give off just before he'd bark. I half woke up and rubbed him behind the ears to try and get him to calm down. It wasn't working. I pulled my .38 out of the nightstand and tiptoed toward the bedroom door. Morton watched but didn't get off the bed. I slowly opened the door and listened, but didn't hear anything.

Morton sat on the bed, watching me as I tiptoed down the hall. I stopped every few feet, listened, and still couldn't hear anything. I looked out the window at the top of the stairs. At this hour the street was dead quiet. I still couldn't pick up any sound and was about to head back to bed when I saw him hurrying down my driveway and across the street. Make that trying to hurry across the street. His right foot looked to be a walking cast, which gave him a decided limp. He had a metal crutch under his right arm. I thought I recognized the crew cut, but just in case I had any doubt, the tattoo wrapped around his left bicep was a dead giveaway. I hustled back to my bedroom, pulled on some jeans, slipped on a pair of shoes, and hurried out the door. I saw a glimpse of him limping his way through the parking lot across the street. Even with the crutch and the walking cast, he was still making pretty good time, oblivious that anyone might be following.

I caught up to him on the far side of the parking lot. He glanced over his shoulder when I stepped on a branch, and it snapped. He tried to pick up speed and ended up falling as he stumbled off the street curb. I was on him before he could get back up.

"Didn't I just leave you like this the other night?" I moved my foot to apply pressure on the walking cast.

"No, no, please don't. Hey look, I didn't mean no harm, I didn't do anything, honest."

"It's just after four in the damn morning. What in the hell are you doing at my place?"

"I think I made a big mistake, I—"

"I'll say, now what in the hell are you doing here?

"I was gonna let the air out of your tires like you did to me, but I didn't, honest. I just want to get out of this town."

"I didn't let the air out of your tires," I said, thinking a puncture was something completely different.

"Well someone did, same night you shot me and gave Cyril that concussion. Had to have the damn thing towed, all four tires were flat."

"Cyril, your pal with the sap. And what's your name?"

"Hilton, Hilton Brady."

"Hilton…that sounds like some kind of hotel."

"Yeah, my ma said she got knocked up at a party in a Hilton and thought the name was kinda classy."

"And where is your pal, Cyril now?" I said, quickly looking around.

"He flew back last night. Doctor told him he shouldn't do a six-hour drive with the concussion. I'm driving back to Chicago just as soon as I can, honest."

"As soon as you can?"

"For real, man, the car's packed. You can even check it if you don't believe me. I'm leaving town."

"What's Hackett pay you guys, anyway?"

"That bastard. He said since we didn't do anything to you, he wasn't going to pay us. Bastard just stiffed the both of us, me and Cyril."

"You do much work for him?"

"No, not really, and believe me, we'll never be doing anything for him ever again. I can promise you that."

"Let me help you up, Hilton," I said, then helped him to his feet and watched him tuck the crutch under his right arm. "You interested in a cup of coffee? I can put a fresh pot on and give you a travel mug to head out of town with."

"Thanks, but to tell you the truth, no offense, I think I'd just like to get on the road and start heading south. Nothing's gone my way ever since we came up here."

"Where you parked? I'll walk you to your car."

"I'm just around the corner here. I can make it fine."

"I'll help you anyway, just to, you know, make sure you're heading south."

"Thanks, it's been quite a stay," he said and began limping toward his car. I could see the Mercury Mountaineer sitting against the curb just a couple of houses away. "We were planning on leaving. We'd done a special job for Mr. Hackett, at least we thought we did. I guess it didn't turn out so well, or so he said. Anyway, we can't afford to stay up here any longer, and we just decided to pull the plug. Then he comes along with this great idea," Hilton nodded at me. "And that didn't really go our way either."

"What was the special job you did for him?"

"Seriously?"

"Yeah, just curious. Believe me, I'm not going to be telling anyone."

"Well, yeah, I suppose you won't. See there was this neighbor of Hackett's, some kind of doctor. Anyway, the wife of this guy had some jewelry that we were supposed to grab, and, well we did. Problem was the stuff turned out to be fake, and Hackett wasn't going to pay us. Then we took on the other project, namely you. That didn't exactly bounce our way either. Now I just want to get my ass back home and maybe catch a Cubs game."

"This jewelry? Was it a diamond necklace about this big?" I held my hands up, overlapping my thumb and index fingers. "Kind of looked like an inverted triangle, and the bottom diamond swung back and forth?"

"Yeah, how'd you know that?"

"I know the woman Hackett gave it to. Those diamonds were real. The thing appraised at about twenty-four grand."

"What?" he shouted, and his voice echoed off the front of the condo building across the street.

"Yeah, twenty-four grand. And you say it's stolen."

"Damn right, it is. We took it, Cyril and me. That bastard Hackett, he's been cheating us all along, right out of the chute."

"Don't feel like the Lone Ranger, Hilton. I'm coming to the conclusion that's how he deals with everyone."

"Really, it's worth twenty-four grand?"

"Yeah, really. He gave it to this woman, and I know it was appraised by a reputable source."

Hilton stood alongside his Mercury Mountaineer with the four recently patched tires and just shook his head. "There's some kind of bad karma when it comes to that Hackett dude. With any luck, I'll be in Chicago by early afternoon, and I'll never, ever have to see him again."

"Have a safe trip."

Thirty-six

I was eating the remainder of last night's taco dinner for breakfast. Morton was lying in a patch of sunlight on the kitchen floor, busily working over the last of his rawhide chew toy, when there was a knock on the front door. I envisioned Hilton Brady needing a place to stay after his Mercury Mountaineer broke down about a mile away. Wrong again. Two guys wearing ties, one of whom, unfortunately, looked vaguely familiar.

"Yes?" I said as I opened the door.

"Devlin Haskell?"

"Yeah."

"Saint Paul Police. We'd like to ask you some questions."

"I know you," I said to the guy in the green checked sport coat. "Richards, is it?"

"Detective Randolph, just like the street," he said and flashed a quick smile. "This is Sergeant Perez. Can we come in?"

"Yeah, sure. How about some coffee? Just made it, it's fresh."

"No, thanks," Randolph said.

"I'll take some," Perez said, and they followed me out to the kitchen.

"That's Morton," I nodded at Morton, who gave just a cursory glance at the two cops before he returned to his chew toy. I attempted to make small talk while running through any number of reasons they were here. Swindle Lawless, shooting Hilton Brady in the foot, assaulting his pal Cyril, breaking into Heidi's house, assaulting Austin Hackett, the expired license tab on my car, the list went on. "So how can I help you gentlemen this morning?" I said, then pushed a full coffee mug over to Sergeant Perez.

"We received a report that you are in possession of an item that had been reported as stolen."

"And what would that be?"

Perez reached into his coat pocket and took out a number ten envelope. He opened the envelope and pulled out a bunch of sheets that were stapled together. The top sheet was a blurry image of a bracelet. By the look of the thing, I guessed it was supposed to be diamonds. Shit.

"This wouldn't happen to look familiar, would it?" Perez said, then took a sip from his coffee mug and winced. "Oh, man."

"Yeah, I like it strong."

"And bad. How 'bout those images?"

"Never seen it," I said, nodding at the image of the bracelet. There was a description beneath the image. The description started with an ID number with a dash at the end and then 001. I guessed it might represent an insurance policy or something. A sentence or two actually described the piece along with a replacement value at the end of the description. The bracelet was valued at twelve grand. "Nope, sorry, but it doesn't look familiar."

"Maybe check the rest," Perez said, then set his barely touched coffee mug on the counter and pushed it back toward me.

I gave a sigh and turned to the next page, which showed a diamond ring featuring one large stone that looked big enough you'd be able to skate across it. The stone was set in white gold. The description at the bottom of the page gave an appraised value of fourteen grand. "Never seen it."

Perez gave an encouraging nod, and I flipped the page to a pair of diamond earrings. They had a hook for a pierced ear instead of a post, and I guessed they would dangle. The stones looked fairly large with an appraised value of forty-five hundred bucks. "Nothing I recall," I said and then flipped the page and stared at Heidi's diamond necklace with an appraised value of thirty grand, about six more than the appraisal I'd gotten. I was screwed, and both cops knew it.

"This is why you're here, isn't it?" I said, and half tossed the images back across the counter to them.

"We received a report that you requested an appraisal of this piece. As you're probably aware, it was stolen along with these other items."

"Actually, I didn't know that. Here's the deal," I said then proceeded to tell my tale of woe. I didn't mention Heidi's name, nor did I mention Hackett, although I really wanted to.

"And your friend received this as a gift from the individual she's seeing?"

"Yeah, like I said, the guy is such a slime ball, and based on what I know about him, I was absolutely convinced that necklace was a fake. No one was more surprised than me when it turned out to be real and worth a lot of dough."

"And you've never seen these other items?"

"No, but my guess is they are somewhere in her very immediate future. Especially that ring. I went to have a chat with her, tell her about all the bad shit this guy has been up to, and if nothing else, try to warn her."

"How'd that work out?" Randolph asked, sounding like he already knew the answer.

"It didn't. She basically threw me out of her office. She has no idea that the necklace is stolen. Hell, I didn't know until just a few hours ago."

"A few hours ago?"

I went on to fill them in on Hilton Brady. I left out his name, forgot to mention the Mercury Mountaineer, or that he was just now theoretically heading back to Chicago. I stayed completely away from the fact that I'd shot him in the foot a couple of nights back and assaulted his pal, Cyril.

"So he's the guy who broke into the house and stole these items?" Perez asked, then shot Detective Randolph a look that suggested this is so screwed up it has to be true.

"Yeah, at least that's what he told me."

"When he stopped by to chat at four in the morning."

"Yeah, exactly. Look, I know for a fact where this necklace is. I'm telling you the truth when I say I've never seen the earrings, the bracelet or that ring. But if this guy operates, like he has in the past, that ring is going to make its presence known in the very near future. I'm only interested in protecting my friend in all this. If I can help you get the necklace back and possibly the ring along with those other two items, would you be willing to give me a little time? I promise I'll work with you. I'll gladly sign something to that effect."

"How much is a little time?" Randolph asked.

"Maybe a week."

"We'll give you forty-eight hours, Haskell. Then all bets are off. After that, we'll arrest you and your lady friend, just for starters."

Thirty-seven

I was in the process of pleading with Heidi's receptionist and getting nowhere.

"I'm sorry, sir, Ms. Bauer is extremely busy at the moment. In fact, she's working on a rather complicated IPO and will be for the entire day. She left strict instructions that she was not to be disturbed under any circumstances."

"IPO?"

"Initial public offering, the stock market," she said slowly, sounding like she was explaining it to an idiot, which in a way I guess she was.

"In other words, she's busy in the event I showed up," I said.

"I'll let her know you stopped by. I'm afraid that's the best I can do."

"Not good enough," I said and headed around her counter toward the door to Heidi's office.

"Sir, please stop or I'm going to call security. Sir? Mr. Haskell?"

Heidi's door suddenly opened, and she stood there staring at me. "It's okay, Kate. I'll deal with this. Come in, Dev," she said, sounding like this was bound to happen sooner or later.

I wanted to stick my tongue out at Kate, the receptionist, but instead, I just walked into Heidi's office and sat down. Fortunately, Heidi took a seat behind her desk then just stared at me for a long moment. Her desktop was cleared of everything except her phone and a photo of she and scumbag Austin Hackett sitting in a big Cabin Cruiser out on a lake somewhere. Her laptop was open, but I could tell it was turned off because the keyboard wasn't illuminated.

"So, what is it this time, Dev? Our last meeting wasn't painful enough for both of us, so you came back for a repeat?"

I noticed she was wearing a dangly set of diamond earrings. They seemed to match what I recalled of the image Detective Randolph and Sergeant Perez had shown me earlier this morning. "Believe me, Heidi, I don't want a repeat of our last meeting. If we can just discuss things, calmly? I'm not going to try and convince you, I know you well enough to realize that won't work. But, if you'd just let me present some facts to you, facts that I can demonstrate, then you can just make up your own mind."

"Discuss things calmly. Like last time?" her voice had already ratcheted up a notch.

"Yeah, I'm not going to yell, I promise."

"I'm not yelling, damn it," she yelled.

"Okay," I said as calmly as I could.

"I'm not able to talk to you now. I've got an appointment in about thirty minutes, and I can't change it."

"An appointment?"

"Dev, honest, I do. Look, I'll meet you, but I just can't talk about all this right now."

"Can we discuss this once you've finished working?"

"Yes, yes, of course." She seemed to be calming down.

"Okay, tell you what, you choose when and where we meet, and I'll be there, fair?"

"I want it to be someplace public, where we'll both feel comfortable."

"I think that makes a lot of sense," I said, although my initial hope of her bedroom still sounded a lot better.

"Remember Il Corvo? We used to have some really fun dinners there," she said, sounding like she was remembering better days.

"And some great nights afterwards," I said.

My comment immediately washed the dreamy look from her eyes, and she refocused on me. "I can meet you there at seven, tomorrow night."

"Tomorrow?" I said, then hoped I'd hid my disappointment, "I'll be there, I'll make a reservation, that quiet corner table, off to the side by the front window. I mean, if that's all right with you."

"Yes, I'd like that, I'll see you at seven, tomorrow, Dev," she said then stood up from her chair. "Now, I really should get back to work."

"Tomorrow, then," I said and held out my hand to her.

She ignored the hand, flashed a quick smile, then stepped from behind her desk and opened the door. "See you then."

"Thanks, Heidi," I said, walked out, and heard the door close behind me.

"How's she doing?" Kate whispered as I walked past. I couldn't hide the surprised look on my face. "I'm really sorry about earlier, but she read me the riot act after the other day. She hasn't been herself for the past month, ever since that creep came into her life. You gotta do something."

"God knows I'm trying."

She glanced at something on her computer screen. "Crap, she's on the phone, probably calling him now. It's like all of a sudden she can't take a pee without asking his permission. He calls her at least a half dozen times during the day, sends her flowers a couple of times a week. She's been filing all sorts of documents for him with his bank. I'm sure for free. It's just really strange. Not the Heidi any of us know," Kate said and lowered her voice. "I think her work's been suffering, too."

"How so?"

"I don't know. You just pick things up, hearing them in the break room, you know."

"Hopefully, she'll listen tomorrow night."

"Good luck with that. If I can help, just let me know."

Thirty-eight

I phoned Nancy Reilly, Hackett's gun-toting ex-wife. She answered almost immediately. "This is Nancy."

"Hi Nancy, this is Dev Haskell."

"I wondered if I'd ever hear from you again. So how's it going?"

"Not too well," I said, then brought her more or less up to speed.

"Unfortunately, not all that surprising. He's worn her down. It's how he operates, and every time she's with him, there's always a positive reward, whether it's flowers or a gift or dinner if she'll just agree to whatever it is he wants. That necklace he presented at the restaurant with accompanying applause is textbook Austin. Anything I can do to help?"

"This is going to sound really weird, but—"

"Oh, yeah, like the rest of the story doesn't already."

"Do you think it might be possible to get a copy of your divorce papers? I mean, I don't know how else to convince her that he's been married three different times. Wouldn't that have given you something to pause and think about when you were going through all this?"

"It would have given me a lot more than a pause. I think I can do better than that. Let me see if I can reach Connie and Marcia. I talked with both of them over the weekend, and I think I can get something from them as well. You're going to need overwhelming evidence. I can email a copy of my decree to you in the next hour or so. What's your email address?"

I gave her my email address, thanked her profusely, and hung up.

"Sounds like she's going to do it," Louie said. He was leaning back in his office chair with his feet up on the picnic table. He held a dog biscuit in his hand, slowly moving it back and forth while Morton sat at rigid attention alongside him. Morton's head moved from side to side, focused on the dog biscuit, and mirroring Louie's movement exactly.

"You know what you should look at?"

"What's that?"

"His house, that mansion."

"I told you, I've already seen the place, big circular drive, a slate roof..."

"Yeah, I know all that, but I mean the financials. You can check and see if he's current on his real estate taxes, that's a no-brainer, it's all public record. But, if you could get information on his mortgage, I mean, if he was in arrears, I know it's a long shot, but that would go a long way in making your case."

"Yeah, good idea. Just let me call around to all the financial institutions and ask for the mortgage records of one of their clients."

"Well, obviously, that's not going to work, but if you could check it out somehow. It might be the thing that gets you over the edge. I mean, basically, you want to come up with enough credible information that it's simply overwhelming, and Heidi will see Hackett for the shit bag he really is. Anyway, start with the property tax information. If that's screwed up, there's a better than even chance the mortgage is, too." He moved the biscuit back and forth again, then flipped it up in the air. Morton grabbed it in mid-flight and had it devoured in about two seconds.

I only heard Morton crunching. I was already focused on my computer screen, pulling up the official Ramsey County property tax records. A moment later, I plugged in Hackett's address.

"God, I don't believe it," I said as the property information was displayed. It gave the legal description of the property, starting as far back as 1851 with something referred to as "The Kelly Farm." "Check this out. The property taxes on that place are thirty-three hundred a month, every month."

"Are they paid?" Louie asked. He was going through the same routine again with Morton and a new biscuit, slowly waving the thing from side to side.

"Doesn't look like they have been."

"So, if he's in arrears on the taxes, that increases the chance that he's not current on his mortgage. And, might that not suggest why he's in hot pursuit of your friend Heidi?"

"He's gonna drain her accounts, and leave her broke like those other women."

"I'd say it's becoming a distinct possibility. The guy had someone steal that jewelry. You said there was a ring in those images the cops showed you?"

"Yeah, he's already given her the necklace and the earrings. That leaves the ring and the bracelet. Nancy Reilly told me she got married about a week after he gave her a ring at the Eiffel tower."

"He could be getting some of that paperwork lined up as we speak," Louie said, then tossed the biscuit to Morton.

My phone rang an hour later, "Haskell Investigations."

"Hi Dev, Nancy Reilly. Say, I just emailed a copy of my divorce decree to you. I spoke with Marcia, and she had a suggestion. We would be happy to meet personally with your friend and answer any and all questions she might have."

"Oh, I don't know that—"

"Believe me, Dev. We do know. You've no idea the hold he can have over her right now. I called Connie, but she didn't answer, which isn't all that surprising. Anyway, I left her a message telling her what was involved.

Hopefully, I'll hear back. Tell you what. When are you meeting with her, your friend?"

"Tomorrow night, dinner at a place we used to go."

"Don't give an answer just now, but at least think about our offer. Not only would it not be a problem, but we would enjoy the opportunity for a modest degree of payback."

"I'll let you know."

Thirty-nine

The more I thought about Nancy Reilly's offer, the more I liked the sound of it. If I could get Nancy at the table, and maybe one of the cops for some added credibility. Then, with a cop at the table, it might just work to have Swindle Lawless and Woofy Barker join us. I was suddenly beginning to feel like I had a pretty good chance of getting Heidi to finally listen to reason.

"You gotta be kidding me," Detective Randolph said. "No, I have absolutely no intention of attending some dinner with you, Haskell, just so you can confront a former girlfriend."

"She's not a former girlfriend, exactly," I said.

"Haskell, she could be your mother for all I care. My answer is still the same. No. Is that clear enough?"

"You sure?"

"Very."

"Maybe Sergeant Perez might consider if I could just—"

"Perez has got better things to do than sort out your failed relationships."

"Okay, what if you let me have your images of that stolen jewelry. It might go a long way in getting it back and nailing the guy ultimately responsible for taking it."

"And if you have those images, you won't be expecting us to join you at this gala dinner event, correct?"

"Yeah, right, well, unless you had a change of heart and wanted—"

"Believe me. We won't. Why don't you give me your email address and I'll send those images to you? And remember, we meant what we said, forty-eight hours, Haskell and then all bets are off, and you're going to find yourself behind bars until we get this mess sorted out."

I phoned Nancy Reilly back. "Nancy, the more I'm thinking about your offer, the more I like the sound of you coming along to add credibility to my presentation."

"We were hoping you'd reconsider, Marcia already booked a flight for late this afternoon, she'll be in just before seven."

"Oh, she doesn't have to do that. I mean your presence will—"

"You're still not listening, Dev. You're going to need all the help you can get, and that's not a reflection on you. It's just that we've been there. We know exactly what she's dealing with. What's her name, by the way?"

"Heidi."

"Well, you've no idea what Heidi's going through. Just think about it, there you are ready to pour cold water on her future, and there's Austin, dangling fancy jew-elry, a big house, the promise of romantic getaways. Which one would you want to take? Course she'll be broke within twenty-four months and ready to jump off the nearest bridge if she ends up with him. But right now, from where she's at, she just can't see it. I don't care how smart she is."

"Thanks, Nancy, call me at anytime. Otherwise, I'll see you at six-thirty at Il Corvo."

"That little Italian place?"

"Yeah, Heidi's joining me around seven. You think a half-hour is enough time for us to go over things be-forehand?"

"More than enough. We'll see you there."

I phoned Tom Connelly next.

"Hi, Tom, Dev Haskell."

"I'm sorry, who?"

"Dev Haskell, we had coffee the other day after you and your wife…"

"Oh yeah, sorry, wasn't ringing a bell there for a moment. What can I do for you?"

"Well, first of all, I wanted to check with you and see if anything had happened on your end."

"With the lawsuit? Yes, and no. Our attorney gave Hackett the word we plan to fight. We're really hoping to get his offer to settle out of court, which we don't plan on doing, by the way. I also brought in a contractor, that front entry will be adjusted for a fraction of what Hackett threatened us with, so that's happening next week. Can't thank you enough for taking the time to talk with us."

"Actually, I've got a favor to ask."

"Oh?"

I went on to explain the situation. I didn't mention Heidi by name. I did mention the interest the police had shown and certain aspects of my conversation with Hilton Brady.

"That's beautiful. He offers to pay these guys to rip the stuff off, then he stiff's them, too? Talk about a loose cannon."

"Yeah, so I'm assembling a group to meet tomorrow night. We're going to talk with my friend. I know she'll listen to reason and turn the jewelry over to the police. They can deal with Mr. Hackett. I should also mention he's in arrears on his property taxes and hopefully, his mortgage, too, although I don't have any confirmation on that last part. Think you'd ever consider joining us and telling her your part of the story."

"Hey, the bastard's in arrears, and I can help send him to jail on another charge. Are you kidding? That's fantastic news. You just made my day. Tell me where and when and I'll be there."

Forty

I phoned Heidi's office the following morning, not that I wanted to talk with Heidi. "Is this Kate?" I asked when the phone was answered.

"Yes?" she didn't sound too sure.

"Kate, this is Heidi's friend, Dev Haskell."

"Pretty generous with that description," she said then added, "Oh, sorry."

"Not a problem."

"Actually, she's in the conference room going over that IPO offering right now. I'm guessing they're going to be in there for a while longer. I can put you into her voice mail or take a message if—"

"Actually, I was hoping I could talk to you for a moment."

"I suppose," she said, not sounding all that sure.

I told her what I wanted her to do then offered to pay her for her time.

"Whoa, not asking for too much, are you. I could lose my job, you know."

"Well, I was thinking if you maybe called from a payphone, told them you were just trying to get a current figure to settle up. I don't need anything like a written statement from them, least I hope I don't."

"God, every bit of common sense tells me I should hang up on you right now, but that Hackett guy has been such a prick. Excuse my French, but he really has been."

"You don't have to convince me. So you'll help me out?"

"Let me see what I can do, no promises, but I'll try, I'll have to do it over my lunch hour."

"God, Kate, I can't thank you enough."

"Just get this creep out of Heidi's life, which will get him out of mine, and that will be more than enough for me. Gotta go," she said and hung up.

I phoned Nancy Reilly next.

"Hi, Dev, thanks for checking in. Marcia and I spent the night getting caught up. I hope we're still on for this evening."

"I just wanted to make sure you were going to be there."

"Believe me, neither one of us would miss this for the world."

Kate phoned me back around two that afternoon. I didn't recognize the number.

"Haskell Investigations?"

"Hi, Dev, Kate. I got that information, wow, worse than I could have imagined. It makes me nervous, just looking at the figures."

"That bad?"

"He hasn't made a payment in over six months, there's a one month grace period, but they're threatening to start legal action on the first of next month if he doesn't bring the mortgage current. There's also a second note of some kind that's out there for five hundred thousand dollars," she said and just let that figure hang out there while she caught her breath. "The woman I spoke with said it'll run over a hundred and fifty thousand to bring his note and the mortgage current. She couldn't give me an exact figure because the interest accrues every day, but they plan to call the note on the fifteenth of next month if it's not current. It sounds like the whole house of cards is about to come down."

"If they're going to start proceedings on the first of next month with the mortgage, that gives him barely two weeks to get control of Heidi's finances."

"What a bastard."

"Yeah, you got that. Listen, Kate, I and a number of other people are sitting down with Heidi tonight, and we're going to lay all this on her, hopefully, get her to see what he's been up to. Would you consider joining us?"

"Me?"

"Yeah, I've got two former wives, a business guy he's suing, documents, maybe two other people he's cheated in the past. You could add that information to the pile. I really want to overwhelm her to the point where it's completely obvious he's just going to take advantage of her, drain her accounts then cast her aside.

We're all going to get together at about 6:30, compare notes, Heidi's due about a half-hour after that."

"Oh, God, I don't know. I'm sorry, but I'm going to have to say no. In fact, I'd really appreciate it if you didn't even mention me. We've got a two and a four-year-old, my husband has been laid off for the last four weeks with no end in sight. If she doesn't go for what you're saying, I'll probably lose my job, and we just can't afford to do that. I'm sorry."

"It's okay, believe me, I get it. Listen, I can't thank you enough for what you've done already."

"Thanks for understanding. Let me give you the exact figures the collections woman gave me. I just hope this is enough to convince her."

"You're not the only one."

I phoned the restaurant, the more I thought about it, the more a table in the main dining room sounded like a very bad idea.

"I wanted to have an informal meeting, approximately a half dozen folks. We'll be having dinner and some wine. Maybe lots of wine."

"We do have a banquet room that can handle up to thirty people."

"Does it have a door that can be closed, so we'd have some privacy? We're going to be discussing some financial matters."

"The banquet room would be perfect. I can assign you a server so you won't have a number of people coming in and out."

"That would be great," I said then gave her my name. I planned to have everyone waiting in the banquet room, I'd meet Heidi in the main restaurant then bring her in, and hopefully, all of us would be able to talk some sense into her. I debated my next move then figured it would be a shame to lose because I hadn't included both of them. Now, I just had to find them.

Forty-one

He wasn't at Wang's or the Poodle, and I was beginning to feel a little desperate, it was almost five. I had to meet everyone in just an hour and a half. I found him at the Yuk Club. Woofy Barker was in the process of trying to convince the bartender his credit was good if only the guy would see fit to pour him a drink. It sounded like it was going to be a pretty tough sell.

"Hey, Woofy, maybe you didn't hear me. No offense or hell, take offense, it don't bother me none. But no. You already owe us money, and I'm not giving you one on the house. Besides, I don't like you anyway, you're always a pain in the ass, so maybe just get out of here."

"I'll have you know I'm a veterinarian, you unpatriotic bastard."

"I think what you mean is you're a veteran, so am I, and the answers still the same, no. Now get out of here before I throw you out."

The Yuk Club was the kind of joint where this was probably a daily conversation, and not always with

Woofy, which probably accounted for no one really paying attention to the current exchange. There was a bulletin board on the wall behind the bar with photos of various patrons apparently passed out. Some had their heads resting on the bar, others in a booth, and a handful of individuals on the floor where it looked like they were simply left and folks hopefully managed to step over them. The sign along the top of the bulletin board read, "One free drink if you make the wall of shame." I looked, but couldn't see Woofy, although there were three or four images where the faces were covered.

"Come on, Andy," Woofy pleaded.

Andy shook his head no and pointed to the door. "Out, Woofy."

"You can't tell me—"

"Out Woofy," he said and continued to point toward the door.

"What's he owe?" I asked.

Andy looked stunned, and Woofy glanced over then slapped me on the back. "Now there you go, my old pal—" He let the rest of his greeting drift off since we were such good friends and he probably couldn't remember my name.

"You're kidding?" Andy said, not quite recovered.

"What's the damage?"

"I'll call it even at twenty bucks."

"I'll give you twenty-five and pour him one more."

"Now, there's the spirit," Woofy said and slapped me on the back.

"Make it a coffee, black."

"What the— come on, pal. Now that's not even funny."

I tossed a twenty and a ten on the bar. Andy snatched the bills up almost before they hit the bar, then tossed a five my way and shoved a mug of coffee toward Woofy.

"This really ain't funny," Woofy said with a disgusted look on his face.

"Drink up, Woofy, we gotta get going."

"Where we off too?"

"A nice dinner, some fine wine, pretty ladies, and it won't cost you a cent. I'd just like you to maybe give a little testimonial is all."

"Testimonial?" he said, sounding wary.

"Tell some folks about your dealing with Austin Hackett, how he screwed you out of the money you were owed."

"He certainly did," Woofy said, then took a sip from his coffee and gasped. "Andy, maybe a little something in there just to make it drinkable."

Andy looked at me with raised eyebrows.

I shook my head no. "Come on Woofy, finish it up. We gotta get going."

Forty-two

Woofy was snoring in the backseat before I'd made it out of the parking lot. Ten minutes later, I pulled in front of the three-story red brick building and parked. Woofy continued to snore and looked to be out cold, so I took a chance and just left him, hoping he'd still be there when I returned.

I hurried up to the door of the building and pushed the buzzer next to number thirteen. I pushed it two more times, each time a little longer than before until finally a voice seemed to groan out. "What?"

"Pepper?"

"Lucky you, baby. Come on up," she said then pushed the security buzzer. The door gave an audible click, I opened it and hurried up to the third floor.

There was a fresh batch of graffiti written on the wall next to her door, although it was so illegible I couldn't read it. She pulled the door open before I'd even finished knocking, then stood there, blowing a blue cloud of smoke over my head, which degenerated into a barking cough. I could almost feel the vibration from her cough standing out in the hall.

"So, back for more, I see," she smiled, exposing teeth yellowed from nicotine. She took hold of my wrist and pulled me inside. "What's it gonna be this time?" she asked, then raised her eyebrows, suggesting God only knew what.

"Actually, Swindle, I mean Pepper, I wanted to invite you to dinner."

"Dinner?"

"Well, actually, more like a party."

"I gotta jump out of a cake or something? Last time I did that, I fell and hit my head on the damn table. They just left me there, and I had to hitchhike home wearing pasties. Got a ride right away…"

"No, there's no cake to jump out of. I wanted you to tell your story about Austin Hackett—"

"That bastard."

"How he was involved with that internet business and was supposed to send you all sorts of customers and…"

"Which I never, ever saw. Not so much as one of them ever called."

"Exactly."

"What's this gonna be worth to you?"

"What?"

"Time is money, lovey. What's in it for your lady?"

"Well, dinner, wine, and of course, knowing that you'll be sticking it to Austin Hackett, plus helping a nice lady get her head screwed on right."

"I look like the happy thoughts, good deed type to you?"

At the moment, she was dressed in tight, leopard skin stretch pants, stiletto heels, and a black low-cut pull-over thing that exposed the sunburst tattoo around her navel.

"Yeah, I can maybe see your point." I glanced at the kitchen clock on the wall above a sink overflowing with dirty dishes. It was already after six. "What's it going to run me, Swindle?"

"It's Pepper now, sweetie, and I'll do whatever you want for fifty bucks and some tequila shots."

"Actually, it's an Italian restaurant."

"Fine, whatever…"

Forty-three

Woofy was still snoring in the backseat when I opened the door, so Swindle could hop in.

"Oh, and what do we have back here?" she said, then slid across the backseat and as close to Woofy as she could get. He grunted and groaned for a couple of seconds, wiggled back and forth, then curled away from her. As I got behind the wheel, her hand was busy searching around in the pocket of his jeans.

"Lots of luck finding any money," I said then drove off. It was still rush-hour traffic, and I was paying attention to my driving. After maybe five minutes, I pulled up at a stoplight and glanced in the rearview mirror. Woofy was the only one visible, but neither rear door had opened, so Swindle had to be back there somewhere. Woofy's eyes were squinted closed, and he had a large smile on his face. Swindle was nowhere to be seen.

"Hey, Swindle, tell me you're not working in the backseat of my car," I said just as the light changed. At this point, Woofy gave off a low groan. "Swindle, what the hell are—" Her hand suddenly reached up from the floor of the backseat and slapped me on the back of the head, and I drove on in silence.

I pulled into the parking lot of Il Corvo and took my time parking. By the time I turned the engine off, Swindle was up, sitting in the far corner of the backseat and staring out the window.

Woofy was wide awake, facing her and ever the charmer, leaning forward in an effort to get as close as possible without being too obvious. "I don't think I caught your name, babe."

"Woofy, get the hell out of my car. You too, Swindle."

"It's Pepper," she barked back, then fired up a cigarette, which, of course, brought on another coughing jag.

"Pepper? You're not the dancer, are you?" Woofy asked.

"Oh, you better believe it, honey," she said, then took a long drag from her cigarette and linked arms with Woofy. "What's your pleasure, baby?"

Woofy gulped audibly, looked a tad bit embarrassed, and said, "I think you already know."

The two of them followed me into the restaurant. There was a relatively small entryway, then another door made of heavy wood planks with a window that was triangular shaped with the sides curving up toward the point at the top. I held the door for the loving couple, then followed them inside and managed to get in front of them just as a woman approached with an armload of menus.

"How many tonight?" She asked then gave a quick glance at Woofy and Swindle standing behind me and seemed to make an even quicker assessment.

"Actually, I have a reservation for the banquet room at 6:30."

"Oh, Mr. Haskell, is it?"

"Yes, that's correct."

"And you're all together?" she asked, sounding a bit confused, indicating Woofy and Swindle with a nod of her chin.

"Yes, we're together," I said.

"Okay," she said, but in a sing-song way that suggested something along the lines of "I hope you know what you're doing." She made a quick notation in a reservation book sitting next to the cash register, then said, "If you'd like to follow me."

We wound our way into the back of the restaurant toward a door with a sign on it that said "Private." She opened the door, stepped inside, and then held the door for us.

"Whoa, pretty damn fancy," Swindle said as she entered arm in arm with Woofy. When she passed me, I noticed her black thong had risen up in the back, maybe two inches above her leopard skin stretch pants.

"I'll have a server join you in just a moment," the receptionist said as she distributed menus around a large round table set up in the middle of the room. A white table cloth was draped almost to the floor, with elegant silverware and a napkin placed in one of the two stemmed glasses set at every place.

"I'd like a drink," Woofy said.

"I'll let your server know," she smiled, then fled the scene.

Tom Connelly arrived a few minutes later. He had a bottle of Peroni, an Italian beer, in his hand. He set an empty glass on the table and proceeded to sip from the bottle. "Hey, Haskell, nice set up." He waved a manila file in his hand. "I brought a copy of the paperwork, just in case someone has any questions. This her?" he asked, nodding at Swindle and sounding more than a little surprised.

"No, just one more person who hasn't had the most positive experience dealing with Austin Hackett. Tom Connelly, this is Swindle Lawless."

"Swindle?"

"Why don't you just call me Pepper, honey. It's a real pleasure to meet you," she said, then unhooked herself from Woofy and stepped in close next to Tom. "Tim?"

"No, Tom, Tom Connelly."

"And Tom, I'd like to introduce Marcel Barker. Marcel, this is Tom Connelly."

"Yeah, hi. Everyone calls me Woofy. Hey, where'd you get that beer, anyway?"

At that moment, a server came in and headed toward us. "May I take your drink order?" he asked. He looked young, maybe early twenties, lean, still somewhat baby-faced. Swindle was giving him the once-over while still standing as close to Tom as possible without actually getting in his pocket.

"Nothing for me," I said.

"Double Jack Daniels, on the rocks," Woofy said.

"Bottle of your best tequila," Swindle said.

"Maybe just a glass of white wine for the lady," I said.

"Don't give me that lady shit, come on, loosen up," Swindle said, then reached down and tried to grab my crotch, which caused me to jump back.

The server looked at me wide-eyed and remained frozen in place.

"I think just the drinks will do for now," I said.

As he opened the door to leave, Nancy Reilly and an attractive brunette I guessed was Marcia Paxton walked in and headed for our small group. Seeing the two women together and being very aware of Heidi's physical characteristics, I could see the commonality between them. Nice figures, well endowed, all approximately five feet five inches tall, and they carried themselves with an air of self-confidence. Not at all haughty, but they held their heads up and looked everyone in the eye. Nancy took my hand and gave me a kiss on the cheek.

"You holding up okay?" she asked.

"Nancy, thanks for coming, and you must be Marcia," I said.

"Nice to meet you, Mr. Haskell."

"Call me, Dev, please. Thank you so much for coming. Thanks to all of you for coming. If we could all take a seat and chat for a few minutes, I expect Heidi will be here shortly. I'd like to just go over what I want to cover."

Forty-four

It seemed to be a no-brainer. Though maybe not as polished as Nancy, Marcia, or Tom Connelly, even Woofy and Swindle had it pretty much together. Now, if I could just keep Woofy away from the Jack Daniels and Swindle away from Tom, I figured we had a pretty good shot at convincing Heidi.

At five minutes before seven, I went and stood next to the receptionist.

"Is there something I could help you with, sir?"

"No, thanks. Actually, I'm just waiting for our final guest. She's always notoriously late, so I wanted to grab her the moment she came in the door."

"Maybe just take that end stool at the bar. What's her name just in case she calls?"

"Bauer, Heidi Bauer."

"If I hear anything I'll let you know, sir."

That was at just a little before seven. At about ten minutes to eight, I was still on the barstool, waiting. I'd phoned Heidi's cell twice, her office once, and her home three times, but always ended up leaving a message.

I caught the receptionist's eye. "I'm sorry to bother you, would you mind if I ran back and checked with my guests? I think I'll have them go ahead and order dinner. I'll be back in just a moment."

"Not a problem, I'll keep an eye out for Miss Bauer."

All heads turned toward me as I entered the banquet room.

"Anything?" Nancy asked.

"Afraid not. She's usually late wherever she goes, but this is getting extreme, even for her."

"I wonder if he got to her," Nancy said, saying it more to Marcia than me.

"It would be just like him to find out."

"But how would he even know? No one here would have talked to him."

"She told him," they said almost together.

'She wouldn't do that, would she?"

"She checked in with him, or more likely, he called her. He's probably calling about every hour and a half, telling her how much he loves her," Nancy said.

"He'll be planning their next big getaway, and then at the last minute something will come up, and they won't be able to go. It's part of the scam. You start thinking he's so dedicated to helping folks you lose sight of the fact that he's leading you down the primrose path," Nancy said.

"But she's not the type of woman to fall for that routine."

The two of them looked at one another, nodded, and said, "She told him."

Then Nancy said, "He probably came and took her from the office, promised something, a trip, Paris, the Bahama's."

"Do you know anyone in her office, someone you could call to see if he was there?"

"God, I just might. Listen, why don't you go ahead and order. I'm going out front just to see if she showed up. I've got a call I can make, too."

"Good luck," they said.

I looked at the receptionist as I sat down on the corner bar stool. She shook her head no, then led a couple to an empty table in the back. I pulled out my phone and called the number Kate had phoned me on earlier that afternoon. I was still in the middle of saying a prayer when she answered. I could hear a child in the background.

"Hello?"

"Hi, Kate, it's Dev Haskell."

"How did it go?"

"It didn't. She hasn't shown, she's over an hour late."

"Damn it, I knew it. Hackett showed up a little before five and was in her office. I left at five, so I don't know how long he was there or if they left together. I'm sorry. I guess I hoped since she had already arranged to be with you that she'd keep the date. God, I'm really sorry, Dev."

"Not your fault, Kate. She's an adult."

"She's gone crazy if you ask me. You want me to call down there? I doubt anyone is around, but I could check."

"No, don't worry about it. I called her office but ended up leaving a message. No answer on her cell or at home. I guess it just wasn't meant to be."

"Oh, creepy. I'm so sorry," she said, then we hung up. I phoned Heidi's cell again but got dumped into her message center after a couple of rings.

Everyone looked up from their meals expectantly as I walked into the banquet room. It must have been written on my face.

"No luck," Tom Connelly said, making a statement rather than asking a question.

"I can't reach her on her cell phone. I've left messages at her home and her office.

"Bastard's gone ahead and grabbed her," Woofy said.

"Sounds like we might just have all night," Swindle said and slid her chair just a little closer to Tom Connelly.

"I have an idea," Marcia said. "If Hackett's still in town, he'll most likely be at home. If his car is in the driveway, he's either there or, he's taken a taxi to the airport."

"But what if he's still working or just out to dinner?" Tom said.

"We know how to check for that, but we should leave now. Every second's going to count at this stage."

Tom cut a large piece of steak and shoved it into his mouth, Woofy drained his drink, and Swindle moved a little closer to Tom.

"We can't all fit in one car. I'll be happy to drive," Nancy said, standing up.

"I got a better idea," I said.

Forty-five

I made a quick phone call.

"Hello?"

"You available?"

"Now? Who is this, anyway?"

"Dev Haskell, calling for some help."

"Help? Everything okay?"

"Here's what I need," I said then explained the situation.

"That's one tall order, man. Okay, I know I owe you. Tell you what you just be ready in twenty minutes. I'm already on my way," he said and hung up.

Richie DeVon showed up driving a white stretch limo wearing his driver's hat, a Minnesota Vikings football jersey, and a pair of shorts.

"Sorry, but it's what I was driving today. A photoshoot all over town for some punk band I never heard of before who promised to mention me on the album. I'm not sure I want that endorsement."

I ushered everyone out the front door and into the limo, then sent Nancy back in to grab Swindle out of the ladies' room.

"Everyone set back there?" Richie asked.

Woofy, Nancy and Marcia sat in the backseat, Marcia had left as much space as possible between her and Woofy. Tom sat opposite the three of them, next to the bar. Swindle seemed to be glued to Tom and had her head resting on his shoulder. I was in the front seat with Richie.

"Just tell me where to go, Dev."

Marcia shouted an address from the backseat, and Richie took off. Twenty minutes later, he pulled up in front of the massive wrought-iron gates to Austin Hackett's mansion. The gates were closed, and there didn't seem to be a light on anywhere in the place.

"That red BMW parked in front of the door belongs to Heidi. They must be in there," I said.

"I don't see Austin's car anywhere," Marcia said.

"Maybe it's in the garage?"

"He never parks in the garage unless it's winter. Likes to advertise the fact that he's got a fancy car, not that anyone cares," Nancy said.

"You think they're in there?"

"I'd say no, but I suppose we could check."

"How?" I asked.

Marcia pulled out her phone and dialed a number. She hung up a moment or two later. "Dumped me into the message center, no one's home."

"You sure? Maybe they're, you know, in bed?"

"Mmm, that sounds fun," Swindle said and snuggled up against Tom.

"Let me get out and check. I'll just climb the fence or something," Tom said.

"I've got a better idea," Nancy said. "Dev, will he recognize your phone number?"

"My phone number?"

"Yes, have you ever phoned him before?"

"No, never."

"Good, call this number," Nancy said and gave me an area code I didn't recognize as local and a phone number.

"Where the hell is that?" I said as I punched in the number.

"Another one of his scams, a phone service actually in Mexico. By the time people catch on, they've already made a month's worth of international calls and get hit with some exorbitant bill. They have to pay it before they can get picked up by a new carrier. Doesn't sound like much, but Austin ends up making a couple of grand a month plus the carrier gives him free service. He's such a putz," Nancy said.

I held up my hand to signal quiet as the phone began ringing. After four or five rings, a male voice answered. "Hello?" I could hear a news report in the background, a radio, or maybe a television. I wasn't sure what to say, so I sat there looking more stupid than usual and didn't say a thing. "Hello? Hello, is anyone there?"

Nancy snapped her fingers, and I handed the phone to her. As I handed the phone back, my hand brushed against Swindle's hair. She let out a little moan and said, "Mmm, so you'd like a piece of me, too."

Nancy put the phone to her ear and a finger to her lips to signal Swindle to be quiet.

"Relax, baby, I've got enough for everyone," Swindle cooed.

"He hung up," Nancy said a moment later. "It was him, definitely him, and he was driving. I could hear the radio."

"How do you know it wasn't the TV? Maybe he's in there, sitting in the dark, and he's got Heidi tied up in the basement or something."

"No, he's got a subscription radio service in his car. That's what he was listening to. Believe me, I've heard it many times before."

"We both have," Marcia added. "Nancy, he's going to the lake place."

"Yeah, Bear Valley."

"Let's all get bare," Swindle said, then kicked off her stiletto heels and tried to climb up on Tom's lap.

"You want to trade places?" Tom asked Woofy.

"Bear Valley? I know that place. Miss Pepper, it's where I took you and those four guys," Richie said.

"Humph, they couldn't keep up," Swindle said, sounding like she was just making a simple statement rather than bragging.

"How far away is it?"

"Normally, about three hours. This time of night, I can get us up there in about two and a half. As long as you promise not to tell Clarence."

"I promise, believe me."

"You know the way if I get turned around up there?" Richie said, looking at Nancy and Marcia in the rearview mirror.

"Oh yeah," Nancy said. "I vowed I'd never set foot up there ever again in my life, but I just might make an exception for this."

"Tom?"

"It would be worth the trip just to see the look on Hackett's face. I just need someone to change seats with me."

Everyone remained very quiet. Marcia and Nancy looked at their shoes. Woofy stared out the window. Swindle moaned then lowered her head down onto Tom's chest.

"I'll trade with you, Tom. You can ride up here in front with Richie."

Once we exchanged places, Richie drove toward the interstate and then headed north. Woofy was snoring within five minutes. Swindle ended up with her head in my lap, but mercifully asleep. Nancy and Marcia chatted quietly, exchanging Austin Hackett stories. None of them very nice.

Forty-Six

Two hours later, we were on a two-lane county road in the middle of some very dark woods. Occasionally we were able to catch the reflection of the full moon off the surface of a lake as we passed.

"Ladies," Richie said. "I'm thinking this is looking pretty familiar. Isn't there a little store or something up here where I turn?"

"Yes, a few more miles," Nancy said. "Actually, it was a one-room schoolhouse, and now I think the county uses it for meetings and a polling place or something."

"I always wanted to look inside there, does it have blackboards and desks?" Marcia said.

"I never took the time to look and see."

The two of them became very quiet as we passed the building a few minutes later. It looked exactly like what a one-room schoolhouse should look like with a little bell tower over the door in the center of the wood-frame structure. There was a county sign out in front of the place. A three-stall garage large enough to accommodate trucks for snow plowing had been built back behind the place. A large pile of sand sat next to the garage, literally dwarfing it.

"Up there, just past that speed limit sign is the road you turn on. You'll want to take a right," Nancy said.

Richie began to slow as he passed the sign posting the speed limit at sixty-five, then made a quick turn to the right onto an unmarked road. The road seemed to just disappear into the dark woods.

"Austin owns the land from about a quarter-mile down this road all the way to the lake. At least that's what he always told me," Marcia said.

"He told me he had plans to put in a golf course and build some condos, do some timeshare lease thing. He promised to name the golf course after me," Nancy said, and half laughed to herself. Marcia reached over and squeezed her hand.

Swindle seemed to adjust to a little more comfortable position. Her head was still in my lap, but thankfully she remained asleep. Woofy was softly curled up in the far corner of the backseat and continued to snore.

"What's next here, ladies?" Richie asked a few minutes later. We'd come to a complete stop, with the headlights illuminating a fork in the road. The road to the right was a lot narrower and looked more like a long driveway. I could just catch the corner of a light blue vehicle and the reflection of what appeared to be a taillight peeking out from behind the trees. To the left, the road seemed to curve down a slight incline. Through the trees, you could see a number of lights coming from a large structure.

"The left one brings you down to the cabin. You can see the lights through the trees there. If he's here, his car will be parked right in front." Nancy said.

"Is there another way out of here?" I asked.

"Not by car. If you drive down the road, you'll see where it opens to a large parking area. It's probably big enough to turn this around. If you park on this drive, you'll block his car in, and he won't be able to get around you."

"Turn your headlights off and creep down the drive, so he doesn't know we're coming," Marcia added.

Richie turned off his headlights and slowly rolled the limo down the incline. Fortunately, the full moon coming through the occasional break in the trees was just bright enough to illuminate the way. I shook Woofy's knee a couple of times with my foot in an effort to wake him up. But all it did was cause him to snort once or twice, curl into a tighter ball, and move as far away from me as possible.

I took hold of Swindle's shoulder and gently shook her. "Swindle, I mean Pepper. We're here. It's time to get up. Come on, Pepper, get up."

She rubbed her face back and forth a few times on my lap and groaned, "I can't get it up. Help yourself." Then rolled over on her back and began snoring.

"Might be best if we just left her," Nancy said.

"Both of them," Marcia added.

Forty-seven

We left Swindle and Woofy asleep in the backseat and gathered around at the rear of the vehicle. Richie's white stretch limo, all shiny and waxed, glistened in the moonlight and seemed to look like a giant banana split.

Nancy had been right; Austin's silver Jaguar was parked out in front of the cabin. Cabin was a generic term. The place was gigantic, made of logs, and lit up like a Christmas tree. The logs were stained a light butternut color beneath what looked like a green roof. Lights appeared to be on in just about every room of all three floors. The third floor featured four dormers, each with a bright light shining out of the window. Smoke rose from the chimney, signaling a fire in the fireplace, although it really didn't feel cool enough to warrant one. A front porch ran the width of the structure with smaller logs arranged in a pattern along the length of the porch, forming a rustic railing. Three large windows sat on either side of the front door.

"I'm open to any ideas," I said.

"We could always just kick the door in," Tom said.

"I don't know it looks pretty solid. I bet the planks are at least three inches thick," Nancy said.

"Actually, I was just kidding."

"I'm thinking, you could just knock on the door," Richie said.

"Yeah, that's got my vote," Marcia added.

"Anyone have a better thought?"

No one did, so we moved as a group across the parking area, around the silver Jaguar, then climbed the massive porch steps made of split logs. The logs on the steps were thick enough that we really didn't make a sound until we were on the porch, and then it was just four quick steps to the entry and the doorbell.

I pushed the doorbell, and we could hear it chime a Big Ben chime that seemed to go on forever. When no one answered, I pushed the doorbell again and waited.

Tom walked over to one of the windows and looked in. "Hey, I can see him, both of them. He's sitting there in front of the fire, just seems to be staring at the flames. That your friend next to him, the dark-haired woman?"

I stepped away from the door and looked in the window. The room was large, with a stone fireplace that rose all the way up to the ceiling. The interior walls were all logs except on either side of the fireplace, where shelves loaded with books rose to the ceiling. A ladder on wheels was attached to both bookcases and pushed into the respective corners of the room.

Hackett sat in a wooden chair in front of the fireplace. His arms rested on the arms of the chair, and he just seemed to stare. Heidi was sitting on one of two brown leather couches with her back to us. I recognized the blonde patches in her dark hair.

"Marcia, ring that doorbell again," I said.

A moment later, we could clearly hear the chimes ringing inside the house. Neither Hackett nor Heidi seemed to move.

"Jesus, you don't think they're dead, do ya?" Tom asked, then looked at me with a worried look on his face.

"Give that doorbell another ring, see if that gets them moving." We heard the chimes a moment later, but Hackett and Heidi continued to just sit there.

"Shit," I said and hurried back to the front door, frantically pushing the doorbell a half-dozen different times. "Come on, come on, answer the damn door, you jackass." Then I reached down, turned the brass knob and the door swung open.

Forty-eight

ancy shot me a quick look, then stepped into the entryway. "Wait a minute, let me go first," I said and held her back. I pulled the .38 out of the holster tucked in my belt and cautiously stepped inside, looking around. I didn't see anyone except Hackett and Heidi seated in the large room.

Heidi glanced over at me, moving just her eyes, then screamed, "Dev, oh, thank God, thank God." She jumped off the couch and ran toward me just as everyone else swarmed in through the front door.

Hackett suddenly turned his head, then shouted, "Get me the hell out of here before that crazy woman comes back. She was insane, an absolute nut case. She—" He suddenly grew very quiet once he saw Nancy and Marcia. His eyes seemed to focus on first one woman, then the other before coming to rest on Tom Connelly. "You have got to be kidding me. If this is your idea of a joke, I'm going to see each and every one of you behind bars. Do you have any idea the trouble—?"

"Shut up, Austin. Just shut the hell up," Nancy shouted. She reached in her handbag and pointed a small handgun at Hackett as she walked toward him. "It is literally taking every ounce of my self-control not to blow what little brains you have all over this rug that I picked out and paid for. So just shut the hell up."

"Now calm down, buttercup, you know how you—
"

"Don't you dare call me that, ever again. I'm not joking, Austin just shut up for once in your miserable, sorry existence. Do you hear me? Shut up, shut up, shut—"

"Nancy, maybe if you just give me that," I said softly, then indicated the pistol in her shaking hand. I could tell she was exerting pressure on the trigger. I didn't know how much further she had to go before it fired, but it couldn't have been very much.

She stared at me for a moment, then exhaled and handed me the pistol.

Hackett seemed to let out a loud sigh.

"Nancy?" Heidi said and shot a quick look at Hackett, then gave a questionable look back toward Nancy. "Were you really married to Austin?"

"I was his last wife, at least that we know of. This is Marcia," Nancy said, taking Marcia by the hand and pulling her closer. "She was married to him before me."

"Oh, this is absolutely insane. Stop it, all of you. Honey, these are nothing but a bunch of two-bit actors attempting, for some unknown reason, to absolutely ruin the best opportunity that you've ever had. Now, I'm within my rights to ask, no, demand, that all of you leave our private home immediately. I don't know what you were paid for this tawdry performance, but I can assure each and every one of you that if you don't leave immediately, you can look forward to your day in court. Now, darling if you don't mind," he said, raising both arms, and for the first time, I realized he was handcuffed to the chair.

"I thought it was a crazy woman who followed us up here. She threatened to kill Austin. Made me handcuff him to that chair and told us if we moved when you rang the doorbell, that she was going to shoot Austin."

"A crazy woman?" I said.

"Connie?" Marcia and Nancy said, almost together.

"Why yes, that was the name she used. She said she'd been married to Austin and that he stole her inheritance. She told me about the two of you," Heidi said and nodded at both Nancy and Marcia. "I didn't know what to think. It all seemed so, so crazy. But now I guess it really is true. Isn't it?"

"We better sit down and talk," Nancy said. "You need to hear what all of us have to say."

"Darling, this is going to be your home, too. I'm not sure what desperate stunt your low-life, former boyfriend is trying to pull here, but the whole thing smacks of insanity. Now, I have a very special little something that will outweigh any nonsense these fools are attempting to tell you. Please," Hackett said, raising his voice. "I'm asking all of you for the last time to leave this home immediately, or I'm going to call the police. Is that clear enough? The police, I mean it."

"Where's your phone, Hackett? I'll dial for you. That very special little something you have for her. Did it look something like this?" I said and pulled the sheets out of my pocket from Detective Randolph with the images of the stolen jewelry. I unfolded them and paged to the image of the diamond bracelet. "Or, maybe you were just going to go for the home run and lay this on her," I said, then flipped the sheet over to the image of the diamond ring.

"Where did you get that? This is simply the most ridiculous bit of..."

"Shut up, or I'm going to give Nancy her gun back. These were all stolen, Heidi. Look, here's an image of that diamond necklace he gave you in the restaurant. Check this one out. The diamond earrings you're wearing right now? They were all stolen from his neighbor's house."

"Karen and Jim Prescott?" Heidi said with a shocked look.

"I'm sure they filed a report, that's public knowledge. Any idiot could have substituted those images for..."

"They were stolen by a guy named Hilton Brady and his friend, Cyril. Hilton's from Chicago. By the way, one more guy you screwed, Hackett."

"He threatened me with a lawsuit," Tom said. "He was going to sue my wife and me for over a hundred grand. I'll be up to code next week for a lot less. He threatens the big suit, then settles out of court and keeps the money. He never does what he says he's going to do. He doesn't help folks; he just screws them. I'm going to love seeing you go to jail, Hackett. That's after they disbar your worthless ass."

"Come sit down and talk with us," Nancy said. Then she and Marcia led Heidi over to the couch and sat down, one on either side of her. Heidi clutched the images of the stolen jewelry in her hand, then looked from Nancy to Marcia as they began to tell their story.

"Come on, let's let the ladies talk. I happen to know where the kitchen is," Richie said, then walked into the adjoining dining room and through a swinging door. Tom and I followed.

"You know," I said about a half-hour later, taking another bite of the deluxe pizza we'd baked. "I should probably wake up Swindle and Woofy. They're still asleep out in the limo.

"Leave 'em," Tom said.

"I'd just as soon those two didn't spend the night in my limo," Richie said. "Remember, there's a bar set up in there."

"Well, just keep her away from me. We're heading back tomorrow morning?" Tom asked.

"That going to work for you?"

"Let me just text the wife and let her know we're working on getting Hackett sent to jail. She'll be fine with it," he said and pulled out his phone and proceeded to send a text message.

"I'll go get those two," I said and stepped outside to wake them.

At first, I thought it might be the trees or maybe the moonlight dimming as some clouds rolled across the sky. But, it was a clear night, and as I approached, all doubt was quickly erased. The stretch limo was definitely rocking, and the windows in the rear were all fogged up.

I opened the rear door and was greeted with a sight I would have just as soon avoided, Woofy and Swindle in a romantic embrace. Woofy was groaning, and Swindle kept moaning, "Oh my God, oh my God, oh my God."

I didn't know what to do, so I did nothing and just stood there looking at the trees in the moonlight as the limo continued to rock. Eventually, Woofy seemed to gasp, and Swindle pushed him off. "Let me just catch my breath, and you can be next," she said.

"No, that's all right. Whenever you're finished, we got some pizza inside, and they've invited us to spend the night. So we'll be heading back tomorrow morning."

"Pizza," Woofy said, quickly rolling onto his back and buckling his jeans.

"Don't know what you're missing," Swindle said.

Forty-nine

Everyone chose a room. Nancy and Marcia settled into a guest room with matching twin beds. Tom took a room on the third floor with a lock on the door. Richie grabbed the room next to him. Woofy and Swindle ended up in the workout room, eyeing a padded bench with straps to tie and metal bars to hang onto. I didn't want to know anything beyond that.

Heidi chose the master suite and proceeded to run a hot bath. "God, I just want a hot soak and some sleep."

I was sitting on the edge of a king-sized bed with black silk sheets. The only light came from a lamp sitting on the bedside table. She stepped in front of me, then reached up and pulled off the diamond earrings dangling from her ears. "You might as well have these. I'll go through Austin's luggage in the morning, or later tonight if I can't sleep. See if I can find the ring and that bracelet. God, how could I have been so stupid, Dev?"

"You weren't stupid, Heidi. You were just," I wanted to say a couple of different things, but figured now was not the time. "You were just lied to."

"I know, but still."

"It's okay. Hey, you're still loved," I said and then stood up and kissed her.

"Thanks. God, you've never said that to me before."

"Oh, Heidi, I didn't—"

"Relax, I'm not holding you to anything. It was just nice to hear it at the end of the worst day of my life."

"But like you just said, it's the end of the day. It's all over. It's behind you."

"Yeah, I guess. Dev?" she said, and lightly rubbed the side of my neck.

"Yeah, Heidi."

"You want a pillow for the couch?"

* * *

The lights were off, and the only illumination came from the dying fire. A small flame crawled up from between the charred wood and licked what was left of one of the logs before it disappeared into the bed of softly glowing coals. I could hear the antique clock on the fireplace mantel ticking as I tossed my pillow onto the far couch, then laid down, and pulled the tiger-skin fleece over me.

"I knew it," Hackett half-whispered in the dim room.

"Hey, guess what? I'm really not interested in anything you have to say."

"They just want to talk about their feelings, right? Oblivious to what a man wants, what a man actually needs. God gave all of them the natural equipment to rule the world. Then with his warped sense of humor, he gave them that female thought process."

"You know, Hackett, I'm guessing based on where you're about to end up that probably isn't something you're going to have to worry about."

"Can I level with you, Dev? Mind if I call you Dev?"

"No, you can't level with me. You haven't leveled with anyone for so damn long I'm sure you've forgotten how. If you ever even knew."

"Suit yourself. It's just that I had a sweetheart deal I was thinking of offering you. You don't want to hear it, want to bust your ass the rest of your life for next to nothing. I guess that's your choice."

"I'm not really interested in any offer you might have, okay? So please just sit there and shut the fuck up."

"Actually, I was going to throw Heidi in, too. I mean, I picked up on the fact that she's still got it for you, knew it the first time we met that night at Desmond's. Remember? I gave her the necklace and…"

"Stolen necklace."

"I knew right then, and there she still had a thing for you. I could feel it in the air. Later that night, she was calling your name in her sleep—"

"Hey, Hackett, shut the hell up."

"That's really the reason we came up here. I wanted to break it to her gently, let her go so she could run back to you. I only wanted both of you to be happy. It's what I want for all of them. I just don't think they ever really knew what was going to make them happy. And if they don't…"

"Will you please, Just. Shut. Up."

"Two hundred and fifty grand, a quarter of a million. It's yours for the taking, Dev. All you've got to do is just let me walk out that door. Simple as that."

"This may come as kind of a surprise to you, Hackett, but you don't have a quarter of a million dollars. You barely have two-quarters of your own to rub together."

"Do I strike you as the kind of guy who wouldn't have a little something set aside just in case of an emergency? My own private little "go to hell" fund."

"You strike me as the kind of guy who hasn't spoken the truth in years."

"Two hundred and fifty thousand dollars, Dev. And no one has to know. It's all yours. No taxes. Could buy a lot of women, one hell of a fun time."

I sat up on the couch and stared at him in the dark. All I could really see was just his silhouette illuminated by the dying coals. He sensed my movement, then shuffled his chair around as best he could and halfway faced me. The clock suddenly chimed, echoing two through the room.

"There, now I've got your attention. Yeah, all that money, and it's in cash, just waiting. All you have to do is unhook these cuffs and let me walk out that door. Won't take but a second or two. Key is right up there on the mantel, next to that clock."

"About the only thing I'm going to do is gag you if you don't shut the hell up."

"Okay, I get it. Not a problem. It's your decision, after all. The thing is, what I've learned about Heidi, money is her aphrodisiac. Yeah. You mention money to her, and she's down on her knees ready—"

I flew off the couch and gave Hackett a solid upper-cut to the tip of his chin, just as hard as I could. His lower jaw snapped audibly against his upper teeth, his eyes rolled up into the back of his head, and he toppled over backward in the chair. His head thumped loudly off the solid oak floor, sounding like someone had just dropped a brick, and then he laid there, very still.

"I hope you didn't kill him, it would ruin all the fun," a voice said from the shadows.

I turned and watched a small woman emerge from the darkness. Her short hair appeared to be grey and seemed to stick out in all directions. Even in the dark, she appeared pale, thin, and frail-looking. She wore loose-fitting jeans and a nondescript blouse with what looked like a hand-knit sweater over the blouse. She kept her hands in the sweater pockets, wrapping the sweater tighter around her although it wasn't the least bit cold.

"I'm Constance, but please, my friends call me Connie. I was married to that bastard once," she said, sounding almost like she was in some other place. She glanced down at Hackett, lying on the floor, and her voice suddenly grew flat and listless. "Hard to believe now, but I actually loved that awful man. Believe me, I've paid for that mistake ever since."

Fifty

I nodded and said, "You're Connie Adams, his first wife."

"Yes, the infamous first wife," she said and smiled a smile meant to be anything but charming. "First, in an ever-growing line of unhappy wives. You're Dev Haskell, the man who's gone to all this trouble. The man who finally decided to do something about this abomination."

"It's nice to meet you. Heidi mentioned you had been here, but with all the excitement and activity, I didn't think to ask much more."

"I was really torn when I got the message from Nancy. On the one hand, I wanted to step in and stop him from destroying yet another woman's life. And on the other hand, I was frightened to death at the mere thought of seeing him again."

"Where did you go?"

"Oh, you mean when you arrived? Actually, the doorbell, well, and all of you on the porch frightened me. I wasn't sure what to do, didn't know if it was the police, or whatever, so I just ran. Still a bit on the crazy side, I guess," she said, then smiled. Her thin lips seemed to disappear as she did so. "Not sure about you, but I could use a glass of wine right about now."

"I'm not exactly sure where he keeps it, but if you know where we could find some, I'll join you."

"What do you say to setting him upright first, then I'll show you?" she said.

"I suppose, just to get him off the floor."

"I'm jealous you got to hit him that hard." She took up a position on the far side of the chair, and together, we raised Hackett back into an upright position. He was beginning to regain consciousness, and he sputtered and coughed. "What a pity, he still appears to be alive. Well, at least he's not going anywhere. What are your plans? Take him back tomorrow and turn him over to the police?"

"Yeah, I'll turn him over to the police along with the stolen jewelry. They'll hold him. Well, unless he can make bail. But it sounds like he's in a bit of financial trouble, so he just might be locked up until his trial."

"But you don't know for sure if that will happen, do you?"

"With the court system, you can never be sure."

She seemed to ponder that for a moment, then said, "Let me show you the wine. One thing about Austin, he knows his wine, and he put in an excellent cellar in the basement. I'll bring you down there, but then I'm going to trust you to choose. Fair enough?"

"More than fair."

She led me out through the dining area, through the swinging door, and into the kitchen. The plates from our pizza dinner were still scattered across the kitchen table, along with a couple of empty beer bottles. She stepped around a corner, then opened a door and flicked on a light switch. "The cellar is down here. He was all about keeping things at a constant temperature and storing the bottles on unfinished wood racks. I tell you, it was enough to make you crazy," she said as she headed down the steps.

The stairs leading down to the basement were industrial steel and painted grey with a raised surface on all the treads. The walls were poured concrete, and the temperature clearly dropped a few degrees as we stepped off the stairs. "That's the wine cellar back there, that black door."

"You're kidding; it looks like a bank vault."

She half-laughed, "That's because it was a bank vault, at least the door was. Some old bank building they made into a hotel or shops or something. They were going to sell the door for scrap, Austin being Austin talked them into selling the door to him, then never bothered to pay the contractor for it. I can still hear the dunning calls asking for payment. Not that Austin ever took a call, or ever intended to pay for that matter."

The door was a good seven feet high, painted black with gold embossing around the doorframe and the name "Archer Security," painted in an arc across the top of the door in gold letters. Just below that was a landscape scene, a valley with lots of trees and a river running through it. A bald eagle was in the middle of the blue sky, holding a banner in its beak with some motto in Latin.

"A little over the top," I said.

"That's Austin. The Latin probably says something like, "What's yours is mine." She took a key hanging from a hook and unlocked the door. The steel door looked about four inches thick and squeaked as she pulled it open. "Wait until you see this," she said, then flicked on the light switch. The floor and ceiling were brick. The rounded ceiling was separated into four distinct bays, all coming together in the center where a star was carved out of stone. Hundreds, or more accurately, thousands of wine bottles lay on their sides in row after row of wooden racks.

"Oh God, it's always the same. I never know what to pick. Why don't you choose? Something perfect for almost three in the morning after an incredibly crazy day."

I stepped into the wine cellar, not knowing where to begin. "I have absolutely no idea. I'm tempted to just look for the most expensive one and—"

The door suddenly slammed closed behind me, and then the lock clicked.

"Connie, Connie? What are you doing?"

"There should be a corkscrew and some glasses in there somewhere, at least there used to be." Her voice was muffled, coming through the walls and the heavy steel door. "I'll leave them a note upstairs. Oh, and it was very nice to meet you."

"Connie, Connie, wait a minute—"

Fifty-one

I thought I heard Heidi's muffled voice. "Dev, Dev? Are you in there?". It was hard to tell between the heavy steel door and the two bottles of wine I'd consumed. They had both been reds, in old bottles, 1985 was the date on the label, and I could only hope they were expensive. "Oh, my God, are you okay?" Heidi asked as she opened the door and saw me lying on the floor. She ran over to my side, knelt down next to me, and cradled my head in her lap. Nancy and Marcia were right behind her.

I remained on the brick floor, slowly moving my head back and forth, trying to get my brain working and wake up.

"God, what did he do to you? Oh no, is that blood on your shirt, sweetheart?"

"I think it's just some wine I spilled."

Heidi drew back, let my head bounce off the brick floor, and changed her tone. "Wine! God, Dev, with all we've got going on, and you decide to end up in here."

"It's not what it seems, I—"

"And you could do with some toothpaste as well as a shower. What in the hell were you thinking of, any-way?"

"I got locked in, Connie was showing me—"

"Connie?" all three women said together.

"Yeah, did you see her, she—"

"Where's Austin?" Heidi said.

"Last time I saw him, he was still handcuffed to that chair in front of the fireplace. Then Connie came out of nowhere, took me down here, and locked me in."

"Did she point that gun at you?"

"Gun?"

"Oh, you, God, I should have known," Heidi groaned.

"What? You mean she's gone?"

"Apparently, and so is Austin."

"Did you search the house?"

"Actually no, we just read the note taped to the kitchen door saying you were down here. Think they're in one of the bedrooms?"

"I doubt it, but we better check," I said, then slowly sat up and groaned.

"Maybe find a toothbrush while you're at it. I mean, your teeth are purple."

Tom and Richie were in separate rooms up on the third floor. Tom wasn't about to unlock his door until he knew for sure who was and wasn't out in the hall. Woofy was asleep on a massage table in the workout room, and Swindle was gagged and tied to the bench meant for sit-ups. Everyone appeared to be okay, but there was no sign of Connie, or for that matter Austin Hackett, although the Jaguar was still parked out in front of the cabin.

Heidi called me into her room while everyone else gathered down in the kitchen. "Here, I found these in Austin's suitcase this morning," she said, then handed me a little blue box with a white ribbon. When I slid the ribbon, the words "Tiffany & Co." appeared across the top of the box. I took the lid off, turned the box upside down, and a black box dropped into the palm of my hand. I snapped the lid open, and there sat the diamond ring, still looking large enough that you could skate across it. She handed me a black velvet bag. "Here's the bracelet, and I put my necklace in there, too. You've still got the earrings, don't you?"

"Yeah, right here," I said, indicating my front pocket.

"As long as you didn't lose them."

"Heidi, I'm sorry things worked out this way. All I wanted to do was make sure you were okay, and the more I learned, the more it seemed you were really headed for trouble. I just wanted you to be safe."

"I'll see you downstairs in a bit," she said.

Fifty-two

Tom wore a long white apron over his shirt and trousers and was busily flipping a dozen pancakes on a large electric griddle. "I'd say, all in all, despite Hackett getting away, it was a successful evening. We saved your sanity," he turned around and nodded at Heidi.

"And we recovered that jewelry," Nancy said.

"And hopefully put the fear of God in Austin, if he's got any sense, and that's an awfully big if, he's in the process of fleeing the country right now," Marcia said.

Swindle swirled her finger in a pool of maple syrup then licked it suggestively as she looked at everyone seated around the table.

"You're sitting in the front seat on the way home," Nancy said.

"Or the trunk," Tom said, setting a fresh stack of pancakes on the table. "Do you think we should call the cops?"

"And tell them what?" I said. "That we broke into Austin's cabin? Kept him handcuffed to a chair, and in the morning, he had the bad manners to escape from us?"

"Yeah, I guess I maybe see your point."

"I think we should all probably just head back home," Richie said. "It's gonna take a good three hours with the rush hour traffic we'll hit once we get closer to the twin cities."

Richie dropped Heidi off first. Her car was still parked in Hackett's driveway up next to the front door.

"Are you gonna be able to get in there?" I asked the wrought-iron gates were still closed.

"I know the code. Maybe just give me a second, make sure he hasn't already changed it. I don't know what else to say other than thank you all for caring enough to save me from, well, from just a very bad situation of my own doing." Heidi started to tear up, but still managed to look everyone in the eye…except for me.

Everyone said thanks and wished her well. Nancy and Marcia gave her a hug and told her they'd be in touch. Swindle grabbed her and gave her a long kiss on the lips, then said, "Want me to come with?"

"No, no, that's really sweet, but I think I just need some alone time," Heidi said, then quickly closed the door and hurried over to the gate. She punched in a code on the keypad mounted on the stone pillar, then turned and gave a thumbs-up as the gates began to swing open.

"I think we'll maybe just wait and make sure she gets in that car and drives back out," Richie said as we watched her hurry to her car. The taillights on the BMW flashed a moment later. She pulled the trunk open, set her suitcase in then turned to give us a final wave. She slid behind the wheel, then flashed her headlights once she made the loop in the circular drive, and headed out through the gates.

"Okay, next stop Il Corvo," Richie said. With the construction on the interstate, it took the better part of a half-hour to get there. Once we arrived, Tom Connelly said thanks, and it would be just fine if we didn't call him next time. Then he hurried out of the limo. Marcia and Nancy each gave me a kiss and told me to call if there was anything they could do.

"She's gonna need some time," Nancy said.

"A lot of time," Marcia added.

Woofy and Swindle smiled, then hopped out and tried to enter the restaurant, surprised to find the door locked at 10:30 in the morning.

"Dev, before you go, no hard feelings or nothing, but I consider myself paid up in full. We're even, okay?"

"No, Richie, we're not even. I owe you big time. You give my best to AJ and tell her I said she's to be very, very good to you."

"Oh, she is, man, she is."

"Thanks, Richie, you're really a true friend."

"You ever need a limo driver or a lawyer, once I pass that Minnesota Bar exam, you be sure to call me."

"It'll be my pleasure, Richie, take care," I said and climbed out of the limo.

"Can I give you two a lift somewhere?" I asked.

"Probably back to where you found me," Woofy said.

"The Yuk Club? Woofy, they were gonna throw you out of there."

"That was yesterday, besides I'm paid in full. Remember?"

"Sounds perfect," Swindle said, then wrapped her arm around Woofy's and ran her tongue along his ear.

Woofy smiled and shrugged at me. I could only hope he knew what he was getting into.

Fifty-three

I hurried home from the Yuk Club to Morton, wondering what nasty mess I'd find. I could have taken my time; he was still sound asleep up in my bed. I heard him groan as I climbed the stairs to the second floor. By the time I walked into the bedroom, he was on the floor stretching like he always did when he first woke up.

I took him for a long walk, then hopped in the shower once I filled his food dish. We were in the office before noon. Louie was gone, but he'd left a note taped to my phone.

"Dev, 9:25. Some guy named Detective Randolph called this morning. Everything okay?"

I phoned Randolph and left a message. He called back no more than ten minutes later.

"Haskell Investigations."

"Times up, Haskell. What do you got for me?"

"Well, I'm not sure."

"Not sure? What the hell is that supposed to mean?"

"I've got the jewelry. I can get that to you right away. I had Hackett, the guy behind stealing the stuff, but he got away. To be honest, I don't know where he is."

"First things first. You said you've got the jewelry? All four pieces?"

"Yes."

"Tell you what, you just bring those down here to us and let me worry about this Hackett character."

"I can have them to you within the hour."

"I'll be waiting."

I thought about phoning Heidi, then almost immediately decided against it. I put Morton in the backseat and headed down to the police station. Randolph was in the lobby about sixty seconds after the desk sergeant announced my presence. He escorted me up to the third floor, then wheeled another desk chair into his purple cubicle so I could sit. His Formica desk was covered with stacks of files. One file was placed in the center of the desk and labeled with a six-digit file number along with the name "Prescott" written in black marker.

Randolph sat down in his desk chair and said, "Have a seat." It was more of a command than an offer, and he didn't bother to look at me as he spoke. He opened the file and seemed to read for a moment, although I had the impression he was just making me wait.

"So," he said, spinning around to face me. "The jewelry."

I'd placed everything in the black velvet bag Heidi had given me, and I handed the bag to him.

"Humf, the Prescott's never mentioned the bag. Let's see," he said more to himself than to me. He turned back to his desk and carefully pulled the jewelry out of the bag, one piece at a time, laying each piece next to the file. He stopped for a moment to examine the blue Tiffany ring box, but never opened it before he set it on his desk next to the other three pieces. He flipped a couple of pages in the file then pulled out the four sheets of paper with the jewelry appraisals and the images. "No mention of the velvet bag or the Tiffany box. Your guy must have added that as window dressing. So, exactly how is it you were able to acquire these items?" he asked. He was bent over the necklace at the moment, examining it with a jeweler's glass.

"I confronted Hackett with the images you gave me. My friend was there, and she immediately gave me the earrings and the necklace. Later, she found the ring and the bracelet and gave me those as well. She had no idea they had been stolen, although she was vaguely aware that the Prescott's had been robbed. She just didn't put the two together."

"And where is Hackett now?"

"I wish I knew. He disappeared sometime in the middle of the night. I'm not sure where he went. I do know he seems to be experiencing some financial difficulties. He's behind in his mortgage and property taxes."

"What's the woman's name?"

"Her name is Heidi Bauer; she lives here in town. I've known her for a lot of years. She has no criminal record, and she is simply just another victim in this situation. Hackett had been courting her, and I believe he was going to give her the ring for an engagement, and then he planned to drain her bank account as soon as they were married. He's done that three previous times and I can provide you with the names of those women if you would like. I'll be willing to testify in court to everything I've just told you."

Randolph eased back in his chair, causing it to squeak. "I had a chat with a contemporary of mine, Haskell. He cautioned me about dealing with you. I have to say I wasn't sure what to expect, but I'm pleasantly surprised."

"I'm guessing that might have been detective Norris Manning, up in homicide. We tend to not get along all that well."

"That's an understatement," Randolph snorted. "By the way, where did this exchange take place?"

"Where? Oh, at Hackett's place."

"You go there often?"

"No, my first time."

"He invited you?"

"No, he did not. I actually went there to confront my friend…"

"This Heidi?"

"Yes, I felt very strongly he was getting ready to give her that ring, and I hoped to convince her he had been less than truthful on a number of issues."

"Apparently, you succeeded."

"I think so, although, in all honesty, she's more than a little brokenhearted."

Randolph just nodded then said, "We may be in touch. I'm going to issue an arrest warrant for Austin Hackett."

Fifty-four

Louie said, "Dev, you've been staring out of those binoculars for the past week." "No one's even out on the street to watch. Why don't you put them down and take Morton for a walk? At least you'll start to accomplish something. And for the love of God, stop that incessant humming, will you?"

"I'm in a reflective mood, Louie. I'm pondering things."

"You're driving me and everyone else who has to deal with you crazy, that's what you're doing."

My phone rang.

"Thank God. Look, whatever job it is, take it," Louie growled. "I can't deal with much more of this."

"Haskell Investigations."

"Mr. Haskell, Detective Randolph. Wondering if you'd have time to chat today."

"Time to chat?"

"Just trying to tie up some loose ends."

"Did you ever get Hackett?"

"As a matter of fact, we did. I could send a squad if you need transportation."

"No, let me get to a stopping point with what I'm working on, and I'll come down. Would the next hour or two work?"

"The next hour will be just fine," Randolph said and hung up.

"Business?" Louie asked, not bothering to look up from his computer.

"I suppose. It was Randolph."

"That grouchy cop?"

"Yeah, said they nabbed Hackett, and he's got a couple of questions."

"I'd better go with you," he said and started to push his chair back.

"Don't Louie. If you show up, he's just going to ask more questions and start thinking somethings wrong. There's nothing I'm really worried about."

"You essentially broke into that jerk's cabin."

"Yeah, I'm sure Hackett's laid a line on him about that. I left Randolph with the impression it all happened at Hackett's mansion, but in the end, I recovered stolen property and turned it over to the cops."

"I still think I better go with you."

"How 'bout I just call you if I need you?"

* * *

Randolph met me in the lobby again. He had to have been waiting just on the other side of the door, he was so fast. "Mr. Haskell, thanks for making the time. Come on

Mike Faricy ◆ 264

up," he said, then punched in a code on the keypad and held the door for me. We walked about ten feet and waited for the elevator. I wasn't really worried until we stepped onto the elevator and he pressed the button for the sixth floor instead of the third floor where his office was located.

"Sixth floor, we getting a room with a view?"

"Hmm, no, like I said on the phone, just trying to tie up some loose ends is all. After you," he said as the doors opened onto the sixth floor.

I stepped off the elevator and there, heading toward us, red-faced and exposing fangs that passed for his smile, was Detective Norris Manning.

"Haskell," he growled. "Can't thank you enough for joining us, you've just made my day. I've reserved interview room three for us, if I recall, it's your favorite. Please, let's get started."

I looked over at Randolph, who just stared down the hallway.

The room featured cinder block walls painted a glossy institutional barf green and smelled of fear and sweat. A four-wheel metal cart was parked in the far corner of the room with all sorts of recording and video equipment stacked up on it. None of the equipment seemed to be turned on from what I could tell. I noticed there wasn't a recording device on the metal-topped table where Manning told me to sit. The table was bolted to the floor, and I slid the bright orange plastic chair back, then pulled it in and rested my arms on the table.

Randolph and Manning pulled two grey padded chairs with chrome legs up to their side of the table. Randolph leaned back just as Manning inched forward in the attack mode.

"So, what's this all about, and why are you here?" I asked Manning, hoping to steal his thunder.

"I'll ask the questions here, Haskell. Let's start with you telling me how you came to acquire this jewelry you turned over to Detective Randolph?" Manning asked. He seemed to be enjoying himself.

"You're working robberies now instead of homicide?"

"I'm not going to tell you again. Just answer the question."

"They were given to me by a friend. Her name is Heidi Bauer. She received them from Austin Hackett, but she turned them over to me once she learned they were stolen."

"And where was this?"

"At Hackett's. Look, you've got all of this information. I gave it to Detective Randolph earlier this week."

"When was the last time you saw Mr. Hackett?"

"The night I received the jewelry. I went to sleep, and he was gone in the morning. I don't know exactly when he left, and I've no idea where he went."

"Do you know where Mr. Hackett might be now?"

"No."

"How well do you know Mr. Hackett?"

"Not well at all. I believe I've only spoken to him two or three times, never a long conversation."

"And yet you know personal information regarding Mr. Hackett."

"I know information that is a matter of public record. He hasn't paid his property taxes, he had at least three former wives who aren't too thrilled with him, and I believe him to be behind in his mortgage payments. I also know that the Office of Lawyers Professional Responsibility, the OLPR is looking into his behavior and that there has been talk of disbarment for at least the past twenty-four months, although the state bar seems incapable of acting in the matter."

"Seems like you know quite a lot for someone who has never ever had a long conversation, as you put it."

"I looked into his background as a matter of interest regarding a friend of mine. It's all public record. Even you could probably find the information. Look, Manning, you guys know all this. What's going on here, Randolph? I told you all this stuff the other day."

Randolph looked at Manning, "Norris?"

"When was the last time you drove up to Hackett's cabin?"

"I've never driven up there," I said, getting very specific with my answers. "I know he has a cabin up north, but I wouldn't be able to find it."

"Norris?" Randolph said this time with a little deeper voice. Manning gave him a quick glance then refocused on me.

"Do you know, does Mr. Hackett like to swim in his lake?"

"Does he like to swim up there? I have no idea. I believe he was a Navy Seal, at least that's what he told my friend. Based on that, he must know how to swim. If you've got him, why don't you ask him?"

"Mr. Hackett washed up on shore yesterday morning," Manning said then watched for my reaction.

I couldn't hide the surprise on my face or in my voice. "Washed up on shore? You mean he's dead? Did he drown?"

"Possibly. His jaw was broken, and he had a nasty bump on the back of his skull. It may have been from a fall off his boat, maybe something else. We don't know at this point. His cabin cruiser was found adrift out in the middle of the lake."

"I never realized you had jurisdiction that far north. How unfortunate, and Hackett was such a nice guy."

Manning stared at me for a long moment, then leaned forward and almost whispered. "Does this strike you as funny, Haskell?"

"No, it strikes me as ironic. If I were you, Manning, I'd see about renting the Xcel Center."

"Why is that?" he said, looking slightly confused.

"Because you're going to need it to hold all the folks who would just love to see Hackett dead. You do some checking; you'll see he was not a very nice guy."

"So, you're happy that he's dead?"

Randolph rolled his eyes and pushed back his chair. "I want to thank you for your time, Mr. Haskell, and your earlier cooperation," he said, then stared back at Manning for a long moment before he stood. Manning's face was quickly changing from pink to crimson, and there seemed to be steam coming off his bald dome. "Come on. We're finished here, I'll show you out," Randolph said.

The elevator was approaching the ground floor with just the two of us aboard, Randolph and myself. "Thanks for bringing our discussion up there to a close, Detective."

"Nothing short of harassment, and I won't be a part of it. I do appreciate your help with the jewelry. If you'd take a bit of advice?"

"Sure."

"I'm not up to speed on the history between you and Detective Manning, but if I were you, I'd tread carefully, very carefully."

Fifty-five

We were watching the rerun of a movie we'd both seen countless times before, The Big Lebowski. The Dude was just in the process of telling Bunny he was going to look for a cash machine when my cellphone rang. The ringtone was set to Adele's, "Someone Like You." Morton gave me a look suggesting the noise was interrupting his concentration. My phone was lying just beneath the wedding invitation for Richie and AJ. I knew who was calling and decided to play it cool.

"Haskell Investigations," I said, then suddenly had a tough time getting another word out.

"Hi, Dev?"

At the sound of her voice, a large lump suddenly formed in my throat, it had been over a month since I'd last seen her. "Heidi?"

"Yeah, I was just wondering what you were up to?"

"Nothing much. Actually, we're, ahem, just watching a movie," I said, trying to get back in control.

"Oh, I'm sorry. Serves me right, I suppose. I didn't realize you were entertaining."

"Relax, it's just Morton."

"Morton? That dog that likes to eat my thongs?"

"Yeah, I got him back a couple of months ago."

"Would it be all right if I swung by tonight to see him?"

"We'd love it."

"Can I bring anything for breakfast?"

THE END

Thank you for taking the time to read **Scam Man**. If you enjoyed the read please tell 2-300 of your closest friends.

Check out the sample of **Foiled.** The next book in the Dev Haskell series.

Sneak Peek

Foiled

Second Edition

MIKE FARICY

One

We were out on Angie's deck sitting in the hot tub, just the two of us. She was a petite little thing of Korean ancestry with jet-black, shoulder-length hair, flashing brown eyes, a delicious little figure, and weighed no more than a hundred and five pounds. That said, I'd met her at my karate class, where she was the instructor. She'd proven on more than one occasion she'd have no problem using me to clean the floor.

We'd been in the hot tub long enough that I was almost through the six-pack of Finnegans Hoppy Shepherd. It's a pretty good beer, so actually, it hadn't taken all that long. I opened the cooler to grab another and realized there was only one left. Then I noticed Angie was still on her first, and as a matter of fact, not even halfway through.

"You're having another?" she asked.

I'd just opened the beer, and the satisfied gasp from the bottle had apparently caught her attention.

"Yeah, I mean, with all the hot water and the jacuzzi, I have to stay hydrated," I joked and took a sip.

She shook her head. She'd been doing that a lot lately. After a moment, she gave a long sigh, like she'd suddenly come to a momentous decision, and stood up. I immediately did a thorough scan of her gorgeous body and set my beer down, ready to welcome her with open arms.

"I'll be back in just a minute," she said and climbed out of the hot tub. She grabbed her towel off the chair and just threw it over her shoulder, not bothering to wrap it around her, a fact I appreciated. I stared as she walked into the house and disappeared from view. She was back two-thirds of a beer later. She stepped onto the deck, grabbed a lawn chair, and dragged it over to the edge of the hot tub.

"You got any beer in the fridge?"

She gave another long sigh, then grabbed the belt on her terrycloth robe and cinched it tighter. Just in case I missed that not-so-subtle hint, she turned off the jacuzzi and the heater. "We need to talk," she said, then sat down in the lawn chair and tightly crossed her legs. Any sense of romance basically evaporated. Past experience warned me that any time a woman said, "We need to talk," it was a safe bet the conversation wasn't going to go my way.

"Dev, you can be really fun… sometimes. No offense, but I'm looking for something a little more stable and a lot more permanent."

"Two words not too often applied to me," I joked.

"I'm aware of that," she said, not seeing the humor. "I thought with a little encouragement, maybe some direction, God forbid a modicum of discipline, you might change. That now appears to be a distinct *im*possibility…" She went on from there, backing up her hypothesis by listing example after example for the next forty-five minutes. I was out of beer. My skin was all wrinkled and prune-like. The hot tub where I'd been relaxing was now just lukewarm. I wasn't sure if I should hit myself over the head with an empty beer bottle or just slip beneath the water.

"…could be really sweet, but I don't want to hang out in bars night after night. Your dog always eats my thongs. It would be nice sometime to go to bed and, I don't know, maybe simply talk about how the day went or something."

"Talk about how the day went?" I didn't get it.

"You know what I mean, Dev?"

Actually, I didn't, or maybe I really did. "So, do I know him?"

"What?"

"I'm guessing you've met someone, and you find him a better fit than me. Right?"

"No." But she said it in a tone that made me think I'd hit a nerve.

I climbed out of the hot tub, grabbed my towel, and wrapped it around my waist. "Give me a minute to get changed, and I'll get out of here."

She just nodded as I slowly made my way to the door, waiting for her to offer an alternative, maybe continue the 'discussion' in the bedroom. She didn't make the offer.

I made my way into her bedroom, pulled on my shorts and t-shirt, slipped my sandals on, and turned off the bedroom light. I peeked out the corner of her bedroom window and watched while she sent a text to someone. At a quarter to twelve on a Wednesday night, I guessed she was letting whoever it was know the deed had been done.

I turned on the kitchen light as I went back out to the deck, alerting her to my approach. Her phone was nowhere to be seen when I stepped onto the deck. "Angie, I'm going to take off, I…"

"I'm sorry, I didn't mean you had to go," she said, then stood up and hurried toward the front door.

I attempted to catch up. "Yeah, I suppose I could hang around and talk about how the day went. But if I hurry, I can get down to The Spot before close. You sure you don't want to come?" I said, then gave her a kiss on the cheek. "See you around."

She held the front door open, and said "Goodbye, Dev, it's been…interesting," as I went out the door. I hadn't taken three steps before the lock snapped shut behind me. I hopped in my car and hurried down to The Spot.

TWO

Morton was in his bed next to my desk, busy working over a new rawhide toy. I'd been studying the girls in the third-floor apartment across the street from my office for the past thirty minutes. Something was up, they had two sleepover guests, possibly sisters. All four of them were in thongs and curlers, sipping champagne, eating coffee cake and applying makeup at just a little after ten in the morning. There must have been music playing, because one of the girls was shaking everything she had while another was singing into her champagne flute and making moves like she was playing Madison Square Garden. At this rate, they'd be lucky if they were still on their feet by noon. I bet none of them were interested in talking about how their day went. I thought about going over there and offering encouragement.

I turned at the sound of someone knocking on the door frame, Morton was too involved with his rawhide to notice. She looked familiar, maybe, but I was blanking on a name. Maybe an even five-four, blonde, blue eyes, nice figure, and silver earrings that dangled a stone. Diamonds, I guessed.

"Hi, Dev, long time no see."

I recognized the space between her front teeth. Bonnie Lowry, from Climax, Minnesota, if I recalled correctly, and given the name, who could forget? I always thought the space between her teeth was cute. She was right on the money with the 'long time no see' remark. I'd met her at a wedding a good ten years ago. A guy I knew had married her sister, Chrissy and Bonnie had been a bridesmaid. She'd first caught my attention standing up on the altar in her bridesmaid's dress, light blue if I remembered, although the dress wasn't what had attracted my attention.

The butterfly tattoo on her back certainly wasn't the only tattoo among the bridesmaids. They all had ink. It's just that Bonnie's butterfly happened to be a well-endowed, anatomically correct, naked woman with butterfly wings. It shouldn't have been surprising, after all, this was a theme wedding, Jack Daniels being the theme. It was one of the few weddings I'd been to where there was a fight. The only wedding I could recall where the fight had been between two bridesmaids, Bonnie, and another girl.

The following morning she couldn't remember what they'd fought about. Actually, she couldn't remember the fight, but then again, she couldn't remember my name, either. I gave her my business card when I drove her home, hoping she'd call. She never did.

"Bonnie Lowry," I said and watched as she strutted toward one of my client chairs.

"Yeah, baby, told you I'd call."

"I just didn't think it would take you ten years."

"You could have called me, the phone works both ways," she said.

"I'd need your number to do that. Remember, that was one of the things you were going to call me about, your phone number."

"Oh, yeah, I suppose. I guess I took a little detour. I got married to a guy for a while, divorced the deadbeat. Got three kids, now."

"Really. Congratulations."

"Yeah, they're pretty good on most days."

"So, what brings you around?"

She glanced at the binoculars I'd set on the desk, then looked over my shoulder and out the window. "I see you're still *investigating*."

"I'm into bird watching."

"Yeah, sure you are. Mind if I sit down?"

"Oh, please, please. You want some coffee?"

"Yeah, I guess I'd take a mug, black. I mean, if you're having some."

The coffee pot was on top of the file cabinet. Fortunately, my officemate, Louie, had left his mug next to the pot. Maybe a half-inch of yesterday's coffee sat in the mug. I stepped into the closet, poured the coffee into the sink, and refilled Louie's mug.

The entire process couldn't have taken more than twenty seconds. By the time I set the mug in front of her,

Bonnie was looking across the street through the binoculars. "I see you're watching large-breasted chickadees," she said, then shook her head and set the binoculars down. She gave me a look as if to say, '*It figures,*' then took a sip of coffee. She grimaced and pushed the mug as far away from her as possible.

"So what can I do for you?"

"I'm not sure, and maybe there's nothing you can do. But I have to try something. I've got a small business."

"Oh?"

"Yeah, started out on the kitchen table a couple of years back, actually one of the many reasons for my divorce. I should back up. I took a bunch of night classes on computers and the internet and then I started going freelance, you know building a website for one business, helping someone else market products, helping another company build a customer base. Anyway, I'm into online action."

"Online action? You putting selfies out there?" I joked.

Suddenly a serious look spread across her face. "I only did that once. Well, okay, maybe a couple of times, but I'll be the first to admit it wasn't my brightest idea. I think there were some beverages involved. How did you see them?"

"Actually, I was just joking, Bonnie."

"Oh, yeah, I ahh, I knew that. Anyway, here's the deal. The people I work with, my clients, are all competing in one way or another with Amazon. So, I've been working to give them, my clients, a higher profile and then, theoretically, more business. It takes a lot of time, and at the end of the day I only have a finite amount of time. Whether it's eight or sixteen hours a day, at some point, I'm limited. See what I'm saying?"

"Maybe, I'm not exactly sure how I would fit in. The last thing you want is me on your computer or marketing your customer's products. I'd drive everyone out of business."

"Actually, that doesn't really surprise me. For the past year, I've been working nights and weekends developing a software product that would make it easy for my customers to do what I'm doing for them now."

"But wait a minute, wouldn't that put you out of business?"

"It would put me out of the business I'm currently in. But I could increase my client base by thousands, millions actually, if I can get people to buy this new software package."

"Sounds great, I wouldn't really have a use for it, but I wish you all success and…"

"Let me finish. I've got a partner, Ignatius Arnold. I want you to watch him."

"Watch him? Are you afraid he's going to rip you off or…?"

"No, no, nothing like that. He's special, a very special person. What I'm trying to say is he doesn't quite relate to the real world. He's brilliant, a computer genius, as a matter of fact. But he has a lot of issues. He's very vulnerable, and I think at least one of my competitors is trying to take advantage of him."

"Is he some kind of nerd?"

"That would be putting it mildly."

Three

I followed Bonnie over to her home so I could meet this Ignatius guy.

Before we left, she told me, "You know how they say a *picture* is worth a thousand words? Well, you meet Iggy just once, and it's like getting the whole book. He's been living in my lower level for the past six months."

Bonnie lived in Woodbury, a suburb due east of St. Paul. It was an uneventful, twelve-minute drive on I-94 from my office to her place. I pulled into the driveway behind her. Her home was a split level that wasn't more than fifteen years old. It had an attached double garage and a soccer net in the front yard with three boys about nine or ten kicking a black and white ball around. What was left of the flowers in the front of the house looked like they'd fallen victim to more than one soccer match, except for about a half-dozen daisies at the far end of the front garden that had somehow managed to survive. Morton popped his head up in the backseat, checked out the kids playing with the soccer ball, and gave a little whine.

"Mom, there's nothing good to eat," the shortest of the three boys said as Bonnie got out of her car. He was

blonde and looked a lot like her, including that space between his two front teeth.

"Then you'll just have to wait for dinner, J.D.,"
Bonnie said and headed for the front door, I had to hurry
to catch up. "This is my friend Mr. Haskell. He's going
to be helping Iggy and me."

"Hi," J.D. said, then focused on lining up his next
kick, ignoring me completely. He gave the ball a boot,
and it sailed over the net and out into the street.

"Come on in and ignore the mess," she said, walking
into the house. I followed.

The entryway was maybe eight by ten feet and covered with black and white tile, I think. There were a half-
dozen Barbie dolls, an odd assortment of shoes, two nerf
guns, a bucket full of legos, a blue windbreaker, what
looked like a broken bicycle lock, and a toy truck scattered around the entry. A short staircase led up to the
main floor, and a carpeted staircase led down to the
closed door on the lower level.

Bonnie headed up the stairs to the main floor, and I
dutifully followed.

"I'll give him a call and let him know we're coming.
You want anything? A coffee? A beer? I think there's a
couple of Cokes left in the fridge. Go ahead and just help
yourself. I'm running to the bathroom."

"I'm fine, don't hurry on my account."

The living room was large, with a peaked ceiling.
The room morphed into a kitchen in one corner separated
by a counter of beige granite. Cereal dishes and milk

glasses were stacked in the sink. A half-filled coffee mug from Las Vegas with lipstick along the edge sat on the end of the kitchen counter.

On the far side of the counter was a dining room table with eight chairs around it and a sticker book featuring whatever the latest Disney movie was. The characters looked familiar, but I was way too out of touch to even guess at the names. At the far end of the dining room table was a sliding door that led out to a fairly large deck. The living room area featured a glass-topped coffee table in front of a chocolate brown 'L' shaped couch. A large flatscreen TV sat on top of a cabinet opposite the couch. A kid's blanket was balled up on the coffee table with three toy trucks parked beneath.

I examined the dozen or so framed photos on the wall. Bonnie, with the three kids, two boys, and a girl. The boy I'd seen playing soccer in the front yard looked to be the oldest. Based on the photos, I guessed the kids might be two years apart. I was examining a picture of Bonnie and the kids at a beach somewhere, clearly not Minnesota. Given the age of her oldest, I think she called him J.D., the photo might have been taken two years ago. After three kids, she still cut a stunning figure in a bikini, although it looked like she'd added a half dozen more tattoos over the years.

"Ignore that photo, I look fat," she said, stepping out of the bathroom.

"You kidding? You look great. I'm guessing this was a couple of years ago?"

"Yeah, Nags Head, really gorgeous. It was shortly after the divorce, and we all needed to get away. It turned out to be just what the doctor ordered, sun, surf, and acting stupid. On the drive home, when we weren't singing Bingo or Old MacDonald Had a Farm, I came up with the idea of a simple link, just one click, to handle everyone's marketing needs. We got back here, and the rest is history. Let me give Iggy a call. He always likes a heads up before I knock on the door. Otherwise, he probably won't answer."

I returned to studying the photos. Bonnie pushed a speed-dial button and started speaking a moment later.

"Yeah, Iggy. Hi, it's Bonnie. No, not a problem. I was thinking pasta, with chicken tonight, interested? No, I know. Okay, hot dogs it is. No, probably not until 5:30. Listen, I've got my friend, Dev Haskell, here. Yeah. No, I don't think so. No, I understand, we'll see you in fifteen minutes. Sure, thanks."

I turned from the photos on the wall. "Everything okay?"

"Yeah, he's just in the middle of something, and he needs some time to get ready."

"Get ready?"

"I think you'll understand once you meet him."

I nodded and turned back to the photos on the wall. "So this is J.D., what's that stand for?"

"Jack Daniels. Actually, it was after that wedding of my sister, Chrissy."

"Your sister?"

"Yeah. I married one of the groomsmen, Wayne. I don't know if you met him that day. I'd been seeing him and, well, we were married about seven months later."

I could have mentioned that she'd spent the night of her sister's wedding with me, but why? "Okay, so Jack Daniels, then you had your daughter," I said, pointing at the little girl in the beach photo.

"Yeah, my sweetie, Stella. And before you ask, yes, she was named after Stella Atrois, the beer. And the baby there, he's the youngest, Bud."

"After Budweiser?" I joked.

"Exactly," she said, not kidding. "The two youngest are at daycare right now. I pick them up around four. You sure you don't want a coffee or something? I'm going to make a fresh pot. We've got a few minutes before we go downstairs."

"Yeah, okay, I'll have some coffee. So, I can't be the first person to ask about the kid's names."

She set the timer on the oven, then pulled the coffee pot out and poured the remnants of the pot into the sink. She filled the pot with water and poured it into the coffee maker. She opened a cabinet and pulled out a coffee filter, placed it in the coffee maker, then pushed a button on a grinder that whirled and ground coffee beans.

Finally she said, "Well, J.D. was a natural, because of the theme at my sister's wedding…"

Once again, I remembered we, she and I, had enjoyed a one-night stand the night of her sister's wedding, but I didn't mention it.

"…Stella seemed like a natural, and she likes it because she's the only Stella in her class. Once we had the first two named, Buddy seemed like a natural. He's a laid back little guy, exactly the type of kid you'd probably call Buddy, anyway. So, we just stayed with the theme and named him Budweiser."

Four

We chatted for a few minutes drinking coffee until the timer on the oven went off with a ding. "Okay," she said, took a sip, then set her mug on the counter. "Let's go introduce you to Iggy." I followed her down the steps toward the front door, then down the carpeted set of steps to the lower level where she knocked on the closed door.

A moment later, a muffled voice from the other side asked, "Who's there?"

Bonnie looked back at me, rolled her eyes, and said, "It's me, Iggy, and Mr. Haskell, the security specialist."

"Just the two of you?"

"Yes."

A lock snapped, and then the door opened. The room was fairly dark, illuminated by a number of computer screens giving off a blueish aura to the areas around them. I counted at least ten screens, all with bits of data and lines of code running across them.

"How's it going?" Bonnie asked, walking into the darkened room.

"Making progress," a voice said from somewhere in the dark, then closed the door behind me.

"Iggy, this is my friend Dev Haskell. We go back a long way. He's the private investigator I told you about."

"Could I see some identification?" a squeaky voice asked.

I waited half a moment for the laugh, signifying a joke, but it didn't happen. "Yeah, sure, will a driver's license do? I've got my VA card, a five-dollar gift card to Target, a…"

"Just the driver's license, please."

I handed him my license. He clicked on a small flashlight, examined the license, flashed the light in my face, and studied me for a moment, then handed the license back to me. "Thank you."

I attempted to regain my vision as he walked toward a bank of computer screens. I could just make out a tall, thin figure who could have been the poster child for the nerd club. He wore glasses in black frames, the kind of frames kids in grade school wore, with very thick lenses. He had an exceptionally high forehead with hair of medium length sticking out at various angles. The hair was anything but trendy, rather more like an eternal bedhead. He wore a Star Wars t-shirt, Luke Skywalker with a lightsaber, with the words 'The Force Awakens' below the image, and a pair of suspenders. I guessed the silver sheet he had wrapped around his shoulders was most likely Mylar. The cap he wore appeared to be tinfoil. I extended my hand, wondering if he'd shake it. He did, although I noted he wore latex gloves and was in desperate need of a shower.

"Bonnie told me you develop software," I said, trying to ignore the weirdness in front of me.

"Yes, yes, I can give you a little demonstration, if you'd like."

"Please, I'd like that," I lied.

"Come over here," he said and hurried toward a bank of three computer screens. At this point, Bonnie was drifting off in the darkness somewhere. Iggy sat down in front of the three screens and indicated a chair next to him. As I sat, I noticed a number of what looked like Star Wars figures scattered around the desk. I could make out a couple of posters on the wall, Star Wars again, I think, but it was too dark in the far recesses of the room to be sure.

"So what we need to do is offer a multi-lingual methodology to our clients with just the touch of a button." He went on from there, rapidly clicking the keyboard as he spoke, although that opening line was about the only thing I understood. It was clear he was in his element, constantly going off on a tangent, maybe mentioning the occasional something to Bonnie, who seemed to understand what was being said. From my point of view, they might as well have been speaking Latin. Fortunately, it was dark enough in the room that neither one could pick up the blank look on my face. After about twenty minutes, there was a pause in the conversation, and Iggy's hands came off the keyboard.

"Very interesting. So, tell me how you envision using my services?" I said.

Iggy gave a slight shrug, rubbed his latex-gloved hands back and forth, and stared into the dark beneath the desk.

"We're about to bring the product online. I can go over funding with you in a bit, suffice to say it's no longer the best kept secret, and we've had, umm, some unwanted interest," Bonnie said.

"There's been a substantial increase in the electro-magnetic field," Iggy added, raising his eyes upward toward his tinfoil hat. "Scanning my brain, most likely attempting to read the code, possibly an effort at mind control, mind reading. It's been increasing steadily for the past six months. I thought things would improve when I moved in here, but they found me. I can't imagine what would happen if I ventured outside."

I nodded like I understood, then looked into the dark where I thought Bonnie was standing. Her voice suddenly sounded about ten feet to the left of where I thought she would be. "Well, as you can see, Iggy, we've got a top-notch private investigator, a real security specialist, on the case so you won't have to worry about it anymore."

"Do you have a relationship with the highway department?" Iggy asked.

"The highway department?"

"Yeah," Bonnie inserted herself. "Iggy's been aware of the efforts of the highway department to read his mind for quite some time. If I recall correctly, you stated in your interview that you had no relationship with them. You do not work for them, and you never have worked for them."

"Yeah, that's right." I nodded, then swiveled my chair to face Iggy and embellished. "I have absolutely no relationship with the highway department, never have, never will." This seemed to bring a smile to his face, and he flashed a mouthful of crooked teeth, suggesting I'd passed the test.

"We'll let you get back to work, Iggy. I just wanted you to meet Dev, so if you see him around, he's just here to help and to keep everyone safe, especially you."

"It was a pleasure to meet you, Mr. Haskell," Iggy said and giggled in a certifiable way.

"The pleasure was all mine, Iggy. Keep up the good work."

"Come on, Dev, I'll show you our files," Bonnie said and suddenly stepped out of the dark.

Iggy followed us to the door, making a weird giggling noise along the way. The moment we stepped out, he closed the door, and then a lock snapped shut.

"You gotta be kidding me," I half-whispered.

"Shhh," Bonnie put a finger to her lips, then pointed upstairs to the main floor.

To be continued...

The way this is shaping up, Bonnie's ex, Wayne, may just be the least of the Dev Haskell's problems. Iggy appears to be a piece of work. You'd better grab a copy of **<u>Foiled</u>** and see how things turn out.

Books by Mike Faricy
Crime Fiction Firsts

A boxset of the first four books in four crime fiction series:

Russian Roulette; Dev Haskell series
Welcome; Jack Dillon Dublin Tales series
Corridor Man; Corridor Man series
Reduced Ransom! Hot Shot series

The following titles comprise the Dev Haskell series:

Russian Roulette: Case 1
Mr. Swirlee: Case 2
Bite Me: Case 3
Bombshell: Case 4
Tutti Frutti: Case 5
Last Shot: Case 6
Ting-A-Ling: Case 7
Crickett: Case 8
Bulldog: Case 9
Double Trouble: Case 10
Yellow Ribbon: Case 11
Dog Gone: Case 12
Scam Man: Case 13
Foiled: Case 14
What Happens in Vegas… Case 15
Art Hound: Case 16
The Office: Case 17

Star Struck: Case 18
International Incident: Case 19
Guest From Hell: Case 20
Art Attack: Case 21
Mystery Man: Case 22
Bow-Wow Rescue: Case 23
Cold Case: Case 24
Cash Up Front: Case 25
Dream House: Case 26
Alley Katz: Case 27
The Big Gamble: Case 28
Bad to the Bone: Case 29
Silencio!: Case 30
Surprise, Surprise: Case 31
Hit & Run: Case 32
Suspect Santa: Case 33
P.I. Apprentice: Case 34
Rebel Without a Clue: Case 35

The following titles are Dev Haskell novellas:
Dollhouse
The Dance
Pixie
Fore!
Twinkle Toes
(*a Dev Haskell short story*)

The following are Dev Haskell Boxsets:
Dev Haskell Boxset 1-3
Dev Haskell Boxset 4-6
Dev Haskell Boxset 7-9
Dev Haskell Boxset 10-12
Dev Haskell Boxset 13-15
Dev Haskell Boxset 16-18
Dev Haskell Boxset 19-21
Dev Haskell Boxset 22-24
Dev Haskell Boxset 25-27
Dev Haskell Boxset 28-30
Dev Haskell Boxset 1-7
Dev Haskell Boxset 8-14
Dev Haskell Boxset 15-19
Dev Haskell Boxset 20-24
Dev Haskell Boxset 25-29

The following titles comprise the Jack Dillon Dublin Tales series:
Welcome
Jack Dillon Dublin Tale 1
Sweet Dreams
Jack Dillon Dublin Tale 2
Mirror Mirror
Jack Dillon Dublin Tale 3
Silver Bullet
Jack Dillon Dublin Tale 4
Fair City Blues
Jack Dillon Dublin Tale 5

Spade Work
Jack Dillon Dublin Tale 6
Madeline Missing
Jack Dillon Dublin Tale 7
Mistaken Identity
Jack Dillon Dublin Tale 8
Picture Perfect
Jack Dillon Dublin Tale 9
Dublin Moon
Jack Dillon Dublin Tale 10
Mystery Woman
Jack Dillon Dublin Tale 11
Second Chance
Jack Dillon Dublin Tale 12
Payback Brother
Jack Dillon Dublin Tale 13
The Heist
Jack Dillon Dublin Tale 14
Jewels To Kill For
Jack Dillon Dublin Tale 15
Retirement Scheme
Jack Dillon Dublin Tale 16
The Collector
Jack Dillon Dublin Tale 17

Jack Dillon Dublin Tales Boxsets:
Jack Dillon Dublin Tales 1-3
Jack Dillon Dublin Tales 4-6
Jack Dillon Dublin Tales 1-5

Jack Dillon Dublin Tales 1-7
Jack Dillon Dublin Tales 6-10

The following titles comprise the Hotshot series;
Reduced Ransom! Second Edition
Finders Keepers! Second Edition
Bankers Hours Second Edition
Chow Down Second Edition
Moonlight Dance Academy Second Edition
Irish Dukes (Fight Card Series)
written under the pseudonym Jack Tunney

The following titles comprise the Corridor Man series:
Corridor Man
Corridor Man 2: Opportunity knocks
Corridor Man 3: The Dungeon
Corridor Man 4: Dead End
Corridor Man 5: Finger
Corridor Man 6: Exit Strategy
Corridor Man 7: Trunk Music
Corridor Man 8: Birthday Boy
Corridor Man 9: Boss Man
Corridor Man 10: Bye Bye Bobby

Corridor Man novellas:
Corridor Man: Valentine
Corridor Man: Auditor
Corridor Man: Howling

Corridor Man: Spa Day

The following are Corridor Man Boxsets:
Corridor Man Boxset 1-3
Corridor Man Boxset 1-5
Corridor Man Boxset 6-9

All books are available on Amazon.com
Thank you!

Contact the author:

- Email: mikefaricyauthor@gmail.com
- Twitter: @Mikefaricybooks
- Facebook: Mike Faricy Author
- Website: http://www.mikefaricybooks.com

Published by

MJF Publishing

www.ingramcontent.com/pod-product-compliance
Lightning Source LLC
Chambersburg PA
CBHW071420200726
48294CB00002B/459